You've connected.

danger.com

@7//Most Wanted/

danger.com

@7//Most Wanted/

by
jordan.cray

Aladdin Paperbacks

VISIT US ON THE WORLD WIDE WEB
www.SimonSaysKids.com/net-scene

First Aladdin Paperbacks edition June 1998

Copyright © 1998 by Jordan Cray

Aladdin Paperbacks
An imprint of Simon & Schuster
Children's Publishing Division
1230 Avenue of the Americas
New York, NY 10020

The text of this book was set in 11.5 point Sabon.
Printed and bound in the United States of America
10 9 8 7 6 5 4 3 2

Library of Congress Cataloging-in-Publication Data
Cray, Jordan.
Most wanted / Jordan Cray. — 1st Aladdin Paperbacks ed.
p.   cm.
Summary: Having found out that he was adopted, Andy
searches for his biological father on the Internet and then
must deal with the consequences of his discoveries.
ISBN 0-689-82040-2 (pbk.)
[1. Fathers and sons—Fiction. 2. Adoption—Fiction. 3.
Mystery and detective stories.] I. Title.
PZ7.C85955Mo   1998
[Fic]—dc21   97-52648
CIP   AC

//prologue

The best decision he'd ever made in his life was not to be bitter. Waste of time.

Hey, people disappoint you. Maybe they betray you. So you get angry. Everyone gets angry. Anger and innocence can go hand in hand.

But people don't understand that. The system stacks up against you. They throw the book at you. More than one book, they throw the freaking law library at you.

Law books—those books weigh something. Man, they hurt when they hit you. *Thud. Thud. Thud.* They knock you to the floor.

A guy can't win against lawyers. Especially when you can't afford the guy in the thousand-dollar suit with the yellow satin tie and matching hankie. The guy who can convince a jury that you're innocent. The guy who believes you.

No, you don't have the jack, so you get some kid right out of law school in a baggy brown suit and a bad haircut who lets the system turn the screws on you, hard.

So, you wind up in jail, and it's not fair. But you get over the feeling fast. Because basically, every louse in jail says he's innocent.

So you say nothing. You watch your back. You learn what you can. You wait. Kind of like life, except you can't go to the grocery store. And who wants to go to the grocery store?

He's not saying waiting was easy. It wasn't. Especially since a whole life was snatched away from him, just like that. A job. A house. A kid.

The kid. Best decision he ever made. Best part of him. His heart was torn out when they took Rocket away. He remembered why he called him Rocket—even at two years old, the kid had a pitching arm. He bought him a baseball mitt, and his wife laughed at him.

But that was another life.

Now, he was concentrating on a fresh start.

And this time, he'd do it right.

you've got mail!

To: whoever@cyberspace.com
From: rcktman (Andy MacFarland)
Subject: blizzard

Sometimes, you can't figure out when something started to happen. Things change, but you can't really say how. Like you and your girlfriend break up, but you don't remember when you started to be bored with her obsession with Brad Pitt. Or you get a D in geometry, and you can't remember when, exactly, you started tuning out the teacher and drawing rocket launchers in your notebook instead.

But me, I can point to the exact day when things changed. I can point to the *exact* minute. I can remember what I was wearing, and what my mom was wearing, and the way her mouth moved, and the way the breeze came through the window and blew all her papers off her desk.

I remember watching the papers drift across the floor. Like snow. Neither one of us made a move to pick them up.

The funny thing is, I live in California. I never had seen snow. But suddenly, I remembered being cold. Falling in a snow-drift. I remembered hands lifting me out, and someone laughing. It was a deep laugh, and it made me happy. The memory was blurry, as though I were seeing the image through the whiteout of a snowstorm.

And while I was thinking all this, at the same time, my world was blowing apart in a completely mellow way. Just a soft voice talking.

And everything changed.

It was like after a blizzard, when you can't recognize your house, or your yard. You know they're still there, underneath the mounds of white. But nothing looks the same. And if you walk outside, you'll sink *down, and maybe the snow will swallow you . . . so you reach out and hold a hand, tightly. A big, strong hand.*

Except I've never been in a blizzard, so how would I know all this?

Look. Here's what I'm saying. If nothing makes sense anymore, you really need something—someone—to believe in. And you'll hang on tight to that person, that idea, just to make everything okay again.

Wouldn't you?

1//blown away

Let me start off by giving you a critical piece of advice for your future—never, under any circumstances, allow yourself to be trapped in a room with five girls and a pile of baby pictures.

"Oooooh! Look at Jason! He's soooooo cute!" Desi Radowitz crooned.

"Eeeeee! Check out Bobby Harrison!" Jessica Rabin let out a high-pitched squeal and tossed the photo to Sarah Grommet.

"Eeeeee!" Sarah squealed.

I checked to see if the classroom windows had shattered. They hadn't.

I had volunteered to help organize baby photos of the junior class for the yearbook and write funny captions for each of them. Now the question was, *Why, why, why?*

"Can we get organized here?" I suggested. "Maybe we should alphabetize—"

"Ewwwwwww!"

I just about jumped to the ceiling. But it was only Winona Bede, who'd come up behind me. "Look at Josh Towney! He looks like a monkey!" Winona cried.

I had this tiny sensitivity to loud noises and shrieks. If someone crept up behind me and went *boo,* I'd go into cardiac arrest. It was one of those embarrassing things about yourself that you don't want anyone to know.

Jessica snatched the photo back. "He does not! He's cute!"

"Eewwwwww," Winona repeated.

"Let me see!" Sarah demanded.

"Hey!" I tried. "We've been here for twenty minutes already, and we haven't even—"

"Eeeeeee! He does look like a monkey!"

Let me stop right here. I'm not dissing girls. These girls are not airheads. They are all probably smarter than me. But get a bunch of girls around baby pictures, and what do you get? Mayhem.

Even my best friend, Sydney Gross, was giggling over the pictures. And Syd is not the giggling type.

Syd held up a picture of Brad Winkler, junior class would-be stud. "Look at this one. Proof that Winkler really is a hound in disguise."

We all looked at the photo and burst out laughing. Baby Brad was a pudgy tyke with the same long face and blond curly hair. He was on all fours and had a ball in his mouth.

Jessica looked up from the picture of Brad. "Hey, where's your picture, MacFarland?"

I pushed over my picture to her. My mom had dug it out of a pile she keeps in a drawer. I had bought her a photo album for Christmas two years ago, and she still hadn't gotten around to putting all her photos in it. Mom is super organized at her business, but our house? Chaos.

When I'd asked for a picture of myself as a baby, Mom had dug into this overstuffed drawer to find her favorite. I guess I was around four or five years old. I had a baseball mitt on one hand that was almost as big as I was. In my other hand was a stuffed dog I'd named Pokey.

Jessica widened her green eyes at me. "Do you miss your yittle stuffed puppy?" she asked in baby talk.

"What are you talking about? I still sleep with him. Every night," I said. Jessica is a goon. But she has coppery hair and some wicked long legs, and all I wanted from life at the moment was to sit next to her at the movies and watch her cross them.

Syd glanced at the picture. "You're pretty old here, Andy," she said. "Everybody else is a baby, and you're almost in school."

"It's symbolic of how incredibly more mature I am than all you guys," I said.

Jessica snorted. "I hope you enjoy being delusional, MacFarland."

"Yeah, dream on," Desi said.

"Really, Andy," Syd said. "Doesn't your mom have any pictures of you as a baby?"

I thought about it. Baby pictures were not high on my agenda. The earliest picture I could remember was me on the first day of kindergarten. Mom is not exactly a shutterbug. She always forgets to buy film, or misplaces the camera.

"Don't you have a baby book?" Winona asked me. "My mom filled this book with pictures of me, and wrote down things like the first time I smiled, or stood up, or ate my first piece of broccoli. . . ."

"Just don't get into potty training, okay?" Syd said. "I think baby books are gooney."

"I have one," Jessica said.

"I have one, too," Desi said. "Except it's only got, like, three pages filled out, because my mom lost interest. I'm the fifth kid. That's what happens in big families. The youngest one gets left out."

"No wonder you need therapy," Syd said. Desi rolled her eyes.

We started to organize the photos and think of captions. But only half of my brain was paying attention. It was like this little noise was *pinging* in my head. Why weren't there any baby pictures of me around the house? Maybe Mom had been too tired to take any. My dad had left about five months after I was born—nice guy, huh?

We hadn't heard from him since.

So Mom had raised me alone pretty much from day one. But suddenly, I started wondering about whether she'd wanted me or not. Her husband had left her because she had a baby. He couldn't handle the responsibility—or the noise. What if she really resented me?

Whoa. Now I needed therapy.

"Mom, where can I find baby pictures of me?"

After the meeting, I tracked Mom down in her office. Maybe I shouldn't say "tracked," as if it were hard. Mom is always in her office. It was five o'clock, and she'd probably still be there for another hour. Mom is partners with Syd's mom, Rachel, in this business called Yellow Crayon. They make CD-ROM games for girls. They were super busy at the moment, but Mom is always home for dinner—even if she has to go back to the office afterward.

Mom looked up. She blinked at me in slow motion. I guess I'd interrupted her train of thought.

"Baby pictures," she repeated.

"Yeah," I said. I leaned a hip against her desk. "We're putting baby pictures of ourselves in the yearbook, remember? The one you gave me is too old. Don't you have one of me when I was little? You know, like, crawling?"

"What's wrong with the one I gave you?" Mom asked. "It's my favorite. You look so cute—"

"I'm just way older than everybody else," I said.

Mom looked down at her papers. She frowned. Then, she looked out the window. "I don't have any pictures of you as a baby," she said softly.

I let out a long breath. "Oh. Look, we don't have to get all psychological here, okay? But did you . . . want me?"

Mom looked at me then. She has very clear, very bright blue eyes. There were tears in them. "I wanted you more than anything in the world, Andy."

"Then why didn't you take pictures of me?" I asked. "Or have a stupid baby book? Was it because Todd left you? Did you think it was my fault?"

"My husband was an idiot," Mom said, pushing at a drawer that was already closed. "That's why he left."

"So why—"

"Andy." Mom dropped her head in her hands. She took a deep breath. Then she looked up. But she didn't look at me. She looked out the window. Her office is in an old house, and there is a backyard with a big, leafy tree. She stared at it.

"I've been debating with myself about telling you something," she said. "Something you should know. It's just that I hate to . . . I told myself that it wasn't something you needed to know. . . ."

She was fumbling, but I didn't say anything. Suddenly, I was very, very scared. Because she looked scared.

She turned and looked at me. "You have to understand how much I love you," she said, her voice wobbly. "When you love someone, when you love your child, the first duty you have is to protect him. It goes deeper than thinking—it's instinct. That's why I waited—"

"Mom! You are truly freaking me out," I said. "Will you just cut to the chase?"

"You're adopted," she said.

Suddenly, there was no floor under my feet. "What?"

"I adopted you," she said. "When you were three years old."

The news trickled down inside me like icy rain. I couldn't move. A gust of wind sent the papers flying. That's when the image of snow came to me. A blizzard, flying in my face, biting into me with cold fingers.

"But . . . wait," I said. "What happened to my real parents?"

I saw Mom flinch at the word "real." But I didn't care.

"Your mother died," she said. Her gaze slid away from mine.

There was more. I knew it. I knew she didn't want to tell me. My face felt hot, and my whole body had started to shake.

"How did she die?" I demanded. "Where is my father? What happened to him?"

She didn't answer.

I pounded on her desk with my fists. "Tell me!"

"He killed her," she whispered.

2//dear old dad

If something really, really bad has ever happened to you, you know how weird reality gets. It's like everything around you suddenly has very, very clear edges. You see everything as if for the first time. You look at your fingers, and you can't believe they're still your fingers. They should look different. *You're* different.

My legs kind of gave way, and I sat down on the chair opposite Mom's desk, like I was on a job interview. She started to come toward me, but I said, "*No!,*" so she sat down again.

"Tell me," I said.

"Andy, you have to understand. I couldn't tell you that you were adopted, because I know you. I knew you'd look for your birth parents. I couldn't lie about who they were, because you could find out. And then you'd hate me worse than ever. So I waited . . . " Mom's voice was a whisper.

"Just tell me!" For the first time in my life, I ordered my mom to do something. "You owe me," I said fiercely.

She nodded. And she told me.

My parents were Silas and Pam Murdoch. They lived in a town called White Cape, in Maine. Silas was a carpenter, a woodworker. They seemed to have a good marriage, but no one knew for sure, because they didn't really have friends. Everyone liked them, but they kept to themselves.

Then one night, Silas called the police, sobbing. His wife was dead. She'd let in a group of teenagers, who had rampaged through the house. They stabbed her. When he got home, he found them still in the house. They ran when they saw him. He grabbed one, but he slashed at Silas, and he lost his grip.

When the police got there, Silas was holding his son—me—in his arms. I was two and a half. I was covered in blood, but

I was fine. Silas had cuts on his arms and hands. Blood was everywhere—on the walls, the floor. And Pam was dead. SATAN was written on the wall. Silas said the kids had quoted from the Bible, twisted words and phrases, as they ran. He didn't know why they'd spared him, or me.

"The police didn't buy it," Mom said. "Not from the very beginning. Neither did the D.A., nor the public. There was no trace of a band of teenagers, no traces of anyone else's blood besides Silas's and Pam's. No fingerprints. Silas said they were wearing gloves and had shaved heads. They arrested him. You were put in foster care because there weren't any relatives."

Mom stopped. "Andy, honey, you look pale. Maybe we should—"

"Just finish," I said.

"Silas went on trial. It looked like an open-and-shut case. But Silas's lawyer did some digging and found out that Pam was having an affair. Or, at least, it appeared that way. She was meeting a man named Ham Jernigan. He testified that they were just friends."

Mom's voice was soft. "But suddenly, Pam was on trial, not Silas. The defense painted her as a needy, clinging woman who was overly trustful of strangers. She was looking for a way out of her marriage, but she didn't have the gumption to leave it. Silas testified that she had let the ruffians into the house because she was so naive and trusting. In other words, Pam wasn't very bright. Well, the jury may not have bought that, but they did think Pam was having an affair. So instead of murder, Silas was convicted of manslaughter. After all, even if he did do it, his wife was cheating on him."

I bent over at the waist and put my head between my legs. It wasn't that I felt faint. I just had to do something, had to move, had to look away from Mom. So I stared at the floor.

"Andy—"

"What happened to me?" I asked.

"I adopted you from foster care," Mom said. "They told me the whole story. I couldn't have a baby, Andy. And I guess I thought having a child would help my marriage—it was a stupid idea. Todd left, but it had nothing to do with you. He stayed so that the adoption would go through. But he was never really your father."

"Yeah," I said. "My father wasn't a louse. He was a homicidal maniac. Lucky me."

There was a short silence. I didn't look up.

"You were such a sweet baby," Mom said. "At first, you cried all night. I didn't care. I wanted a baby so much. And when I saw your face for the first time, I knew exactly who I was waiting for. I was waiting for you. You were my greatest gift, Andy."

But Andy wasn't my name, was it?

"What was my name?" I asked, sitting up again. "What did they call me?"

"Greg," Mom answered. "Greg Murdoch was your name."

Greg Murdoch. It was the name of a stranger, someone I didn't know. But it was me.

Mom's eyes were scared. I can always read what she is thinking. Her expressions are so plain, her eyes so clear. You wouldn't think that face, and the curly red hair and the lopsided smile and the clear blue eyes, could lie, could you? Day after day after day. . . .

"Andy, honey," Mom said nervously. "I know you're upset. But can you understand that—"

I stood up, and the chair fell over. "No," I said. "I can't understand. You lied to me, every single day of my life. I'm sixteen years old! When were you going to tell me?"

"Think about it, Andy," Mom said. "Think about how devastating I knew it was going to be. You just heard that your father is a murderer! That he killed your mother! How could I bear to tell you that? Why should you *ever* have to hear it?"

"Because it's the truth!" I shouted. "And aren't you the one who told me, all my life, to tell the truth? If I stole a cookie, or pretended to be six feet when I'm only five ten—*Tell the truth, Andy,*" I mimicked in a high-pitched voice. "*It's always simpler that way.* You're a hypocrite!"

Mom's eyes went dim, the way they do when she's hurt.

And I didn't care. Not one bit.

I stood over her. She seemed to shrink in the chair, shrink into herself.

"I'll never trust you again," I said. "Never. *Wendy.*" I flung her name in her face because I couldn't call her Mom. Wouldn't.

She flinched, as if I'd slapped her. I wished I could have slapped her. I wished I could be that bad. That evil.

Just like Dad.

3//rock my world

A few days later, I cycled to my favorite spot to chill out. It was a concrete embankment underneath the freeway overpass.

I know, I know. I live in Northern California. Around our town I can hike in hills dotted with wildflowers. If I'm feeling truly energetic, I can even cycle to the coast. But instead, I sit underneath twenty tons of concrete and steel.

What can I say? I like the noise of the wheels overhead. I like thinking of people going places. So sue me. The noise makes all the bad stuff in my head settle down to a dull roar. Then I concentrate until it's a whisper. *Pssssst . . . your father is a cold-blooded killer. . . . psssst . . . your life is a big fat zero. . . .*

"Hey!"

The voice came out of nowhere, and I jackknifed to my feet, my heart pounding. But it was only Syd.

"Oh, sorry," she said, parking her bike. "I know how freaked you get when people sneak up."

"I'm not freaked," I said, sitting down again.

"Sure." Syd sat down next to me. "Beanhead, you've got to stop this."

"Stop what?" I said.

"This," she said. "The Moms are really worried."

We call Wendy and Rachel the Moms. "I don't have a mom," I said.

Syd said nothing. That's Syd. She never rises to the bait. She never tells you what you already know. She never coddles you that way. Which is good and bad, depending on your mood that particular day.

Considering my mood right then? She should have tried a little tenderness.

"Leave me alone, will you?" I said. "I didn't come here to have company. Obviously."

Syd didn't get huffy. She just blinked at me. She has dark gray eyes the color of a sky that's just getting ready to storm. She has short black hair that sticks up from running her hands through it every five seconds. She has very pale, pale milky skin, and a couple of freckles on her nose. From a couple of blocks away, you might think she's a boy, because she's so slender. It doesn't help that she buys most of her clothes in the boys' department.

From close up, you might think she was an irritating, *obnoxious* boy.

"I'm not going anywhere," she said. "Know why?"

I didn't answer. Two could play at that game.

"Because you don't want me to." Syd tucked her knees up under her chin and hugged them.

"You're going to sit here until I talk to you, aren't you?" I said.

"I'm your best friend, Andy," Syd said.

Well, I couldn't argue with that. Syd and I had bonded, big time. At first, it was just because we spent so much time together.

When our mothers were starting the business, they couldn't afford baby-sitters, so they'd park me and Syd together. They'd watch us play ball, or swing on swings, while they plotted and planned.

Then Syd and I got older, and we still spent time together. We knew each other inside and out. And we still liked each other. You can't say that about many people you meet in life.

We listened to the sound of tires over our heads for a few minutes. It had rained earlier, and the tires made a *swish swish* sound.

"You could have told me," she said. "I had to hear it from Mom. I've e-mailed you every night, and you haven't answered. And you've totally avoided me at school."

"I wasn't ready to talk about it," I said gloomily. "And I can't believe everybody knows! You'd think Mom—Wendy—could keep a secret."

"Don't be a jerk," Syd said impatiently. "*Everybody* doesn't know. Just me and Mom. And we're family."

Rachel and Syd really were the only family I had.

Until now.

"The reason I wish you'd told me," Syd continued, "is because I had to listen to Mom's version. Which meant I had to hear all about spiritual growth and Zen consciousness and past lives. . . . "

I laughed softly. Syd's mom is a bit of a New Age yo-yo. So is Syd, actually. But she won't admit it.

"So I'd like to hear your side," she said.

"My side? I don't have a side," I said. "I only have the truth, which my mother conveniently forgot to tell me my whole life. I'm adopted. My father is a homicidal maniac who murdered my mother. What a swell family tree. Got a hatchet?"

"They didn't raise you," Syd said. "Wendy did."

"Great. Born from a murderer, raised by a liar. It's amazing I'm not in reform school already."

"Wendy must have had it pretty tough," Syd said.

"*She* had it tough?"

"Just think about it, Beanhead. She adopts this baby, knowing who his father was. She raises him, loves him, sacrifices for him . . . all the while knowing that sooner or later, the secret has to come out and hurt the kid. So she puts off telling him, day by day. She waits until he's mature enough to understand it. Old enough so he won't completely freak out, grounded enough so that he won't hate her. Days turn into years. And then she tells him because she has to. She's not prepared. Maybe she even does it wrong. And all her worst fears come true," Syd ended.

"She deserves it," I said.

"Mom says that you won't call Wendy 'Mom' anymore," Syd said.

"She's not my mom," I said.

Syd sighed. "It's not like you not to forgive someone."

"Maybe nobody's been this bad to me before," I said. "You don't know how I feel, Syd!"

Syd nodded several times, staring at her high-tops. "No, I don't."

"I can't stop thinking about it," I said. It started to rain again, a fine mist, but we were protected under the overpass. The *swish swish* over our heads went on steadily, like the beat in a dance mix. "The murder. When she realized it was going to happen. When he lost control."

"Andy—"

I gripped my knees. "And I think—do my hands look like his? My face? Do I have the face of a murderer? So I look in the mirror and I wonder—who am I, anyway?"

"You're still Andy," Syd said.

I hardly heard her. "And then sometimes I think—maybe he's not guilty. Maybe he was telling the truth. Maybe a group of kids *did* do it—there's so many crazy people in the world. What if he had a lousy lawyer? He didn't have any money, so he probably had some court-appointed attorney with too many cases—"

"You watch too much TV," Syd said.

"But how do I know?" I said. "Wendy just told me the bare facts. What about all the details? Wendy said that he agreed to the adoption. He signed the papers. But what if he regrets it now? There's so much I want to know, Syd."

She hugged her knees. "Then find out. Start asking questions."

I lay back against the concrete slope. The hard surface felt good against my skull. "Easy to say. Maybe even easy to do. But the hard part is —"

"Getting the answers," Syd finished. She slipped her hand into mine.

Mom poked her head in my room later that day. "Spaghetti okay for dinner?"

I didn't take my eyes from the computer screen. "Fine."

"With garlic bread?"

"If you want, Wendy. Whatever."

She stood in the doorway. I didn't even glance up.

"Andy, you don't have to forgive me," she said quietly. "I know I hurt you very much. But could you please stop calling me Wendy? And could you please look at me?"

So I looked at her. She was not looking her best, let me say. She probably hadn't been sleeping. Adults look so lousy when they don't sleep. Her eyes were puffy, and they weren't the crystal blue I knew. Her red hair was just scraped back in a ponytail. She was wearing an old purple T-shirt with white corduroy jeans that had the nap rubbed away, they were so old. She'd gone to work that way. It wasn't like her.

I felt sorry for her. But at the same time, I was looking at her face, and I realized that we didn't look alike at all. And I got angry all over again.

"I know you hate this idea," Mom said, "but maybe if you saw a therapist a few times—"

"Wait a second," I said. I twirled around on my desk chair to face her. "I found out I was adopted and that my dad is a murderer. I got upset. Does that behavior seem *inappropriate* to you, Wendy?"

She flinched. "Of course it's appropriate. But a therapist could help you process your feelings—"

"My *feelings* are processing fine, thank you. I'm not the one with the problem," I said. "I'm not the one who killed, or lied—"

She closed her eyes for a second and leaned against the door frame. "Andy, if you could just . . . go through the motions of politeness right now, I'd really appreciate it."

She looked truly exhausted now. I knew

why. A family crisis couldn't come at a worse time for her. A major software company—the mondo ImagiTech, if you can believe it—was interested in buying out Yellow Crayon. Mom and Rachel were trying to decide if they should sell. They'd been agonizing for weeks, and had even included Syd and me in the decision.

It would mean some sweet money. Mom could pay off the house, and clear her debts, and we'd still have a huge chunk left. And Mom and Rachel would still run Yellow Crayon—except their boss would be the head of the software company. So even though they were promised independence, they didn't expect it. Not the way they'd had it.

Mom and Rachel had been secretaries at IBM ten years ago. When they got tired of knowing more than their bosses—and being paid a lot less—they formulated this plan to start their own computer company. They took courses, read books, and they focused on CD-ROMs, back when nobody was really sure how CD-ROMs were going to work.

They'd struggled for years and years, and now, finally, the company was turning a profit. But ImagiTech was offering major bucks.

Now for the downside. Not only would the Moms lose their independence, we'd all have to move south to San Jose. Syd and I still had a year of high school to go. I didn't want to move out of Verona. I didn't want Mom to sell the company. I wanted everything to stay the same.

"Things change," Syd always tells me. "Study your Buddhist philosophy, Andy."

"I keep meaning to do that," I'd say.

But now, I didn't care if the Moms sold the company or not. I didn't care if I had to leave this house, this town. I didn't care about this particular life anymore. It wasn't my life anymore. It was a lie.

So I turned away from Mom and looked back at my computer. "Sorry you have to have an emotional crisis while you're so busy at work," I said sarcastically. "The next time my life falls apart, I'll check your schedule first."

"That wasn't what I—"

"Do you mind?" I interrupted. "I really have to finish this."

I kept my gaze on the computer screen. In another minute, the door softly closed. I let out the breath I'd been holding.

It made me feel guilty, being so mean to Mom. But you know what? It made me feel good, too.

I went back to the newspaper archives I was searching. I decided to start with the Maine papers, then try Boston and New York. I typed in "Silas Murdoch" in the "search" box. There were sixteen articles. I printed out all the articles, then accessed the Boston paper. I printed out the eight articles. In the New York paper, I found three articles and printed them out.

I tried a news magazine that has archives online, and I found an article from only last year called "Did They Do It?"

Then I flopped on my bed and started reading. I decided to start from the beginning. I wrote down the name of Silas's lawyer, the opposing counsel, the town where Ham Jernigan last lived. I wrote down the judge's name. I didn't know what I was going to do with the information, but seeing it spelled out on my yellow legal pad made me feel better, somehow. As if I could make sense of it if I studied it long enough, like algebra.

I downloaded a picture of Silas from an article. I stared at it for a long time. It was indistinct and blurry. I couldn't really tell what he looked like. It was taken on the steps outside of court. He was wearing a suit, but it looked too small. His hair was lighter than mine, and I was sure that I was taller than he was. His face seemed just . . . regular. Not handsome, but nice looking, I guess. Regular features. The kind of face that people might forget, might have trouble putting a name to, even if they met him a couple of times.

Nobody special. Like me, after all.

I finally turned to the most current article, "Did They Do It?" It was basically a rehash of what I'd already read. Except for one tiny fact.

Silas had done his time. He'd been released.

Dear old Dad was on the loose.

4//danger next door

I stared at the words. I tried to make sense of the fact of it. It's funny how, if you think about convicted murderers, you figure that they're still in jail. But they serve fifteen years, or even less, and then they get out. They walk around. They have a life again.

I reached for the phone and called Syd. She answered, and I didn't even say hello.

"He's out," I said. "He's not in jail anymore."

"How do you know?" Syd asked.

"I looked it up," I said. "He's out there."

There was a pause. "Okay. What difference does it make?" Syd asked. "It's not like you want to meet the guy."

There was another pause. A longer one.

"Do you?" she asked.

"No," I said. "But I'm still curious about him. Where does he live? What does he do?" *Does he ever think about me?* I wanted to say.

"Okay," Syd said. I could almost hear her brain buzzing over the phone line. That's why I called her—I needed Syd's logic. Her will. Her take-no-prisoners approach to life. She was my Xena.

"If you really want to know about him, I know how to find out," Syd finally said. "I'll go with you, if you want."

"Go with me? Where?"

"To Dolores," she said.

I sighed. "Oy. Do I have to?"

"It's the only way."

Everyone in Verona knew Dolores Sakonnet. Probably most people in Northern California did, and maybe a whole bunch of people in the United States. Parents whose kids have been kidnapped and killed, wives whose husbands have been knifed by strangers, husbands whose wives have been car-jacked by criminals, then shot and left to die. Anyone who has lost someone they loved to a terrible, awful crime.

Ten years ago, Dolores's eight-year-old son Christopher was abducted by a stranger after swimming practice. Dolores arrived to pick him up, and he was gone. One of the other kids had seen him talking to a tall, bearded man near the parking lot.

They found his body a week later in the woods.

A month later, they arrested a man up in Oregon for speeding. He was a career criminal, out on parole. He had kidnapped a kid once before. They found tons of evidence in the truck, and his skin matched the skin they'd scraped from under Christopher's fingernails.

There was a trial, and a total media circus right in Verona. I was only six years old at the time, but I remember Syd and I being totally freaked by the whole thing, afraid some bad man would pop into our bedrooms and snatch us. But the whole population of Verona turned into baby-sitters that summer. You couldn't wander away from your mom for a second without someone asking you if you were lost.

The fact that the man was out on parole made everyone ballistic. Dolores marched up to every microphone she could find and wailed out her grief and anger, and people listened. She became this weird kind of media star, The Grieving Mother. Even after the conviction, whenever there was a senseless crime, the media called up Dolores for an opinion.

But after a while, the microphones went away. Dolores had a breakdown. She went away for six months and came back changed. Over the years, she'd gotten more eccentric and weird. Her hair turned completely gray, and she left it long, hanging to the middle of her back, tied with a suede thong. She started a newsletter called *The Danger Next Door* and distributed it for free. In it, she listed any criminals who had been recently paroled.

Nobody listened much to Dolores anymore. She was just too strange. She talked too much, and too loudly. She stuffed everyone's mailboxes with warnings and called for town meetings every other week. Friend after friend dropped away, and Dolores became pretty much a loner, ranting about how unsafe the world is and how everyone should protect themselves against the hordes of criminal minds ready to kill and maim.

When I was a kid, you didn't hear anyone mention Dolores in a sentence without the word "brave" attached. Now, people shook their heads sadly and said, "poor Dolores." Some of the kids even made fun of her.

So it wasn't as though calling on Dolores would be a fun-filled social occasion.

But Sid was right: I didn't have a choice.

Dolores lived on a dead end. Her white frame house is at the very end of the street. It stands apart from all the other houses, and its back lawn runs right up to the dark, tangled woods.

"Whoa, totally symbolic," Syd said in a low tone. "Ms. Tomason would flip." Ms. Tomason is our English teacher. She can go on for months about the symbolism in some moldy old novel like *The Scarlet Letter*.

We felt a little nervous about knocking,

but we'd come too far now. I saw a curtain flicker, and I knew Dolores was watching us.

"We'd better knock before she shoots us," I muttered.

We knocked on the door, and a second later, it opened. Dolores peered around the chain.

"Dolores, it's Andy MacFarland and Syd Gross," I said. "You know us, right? We think we need your help."

"Our mothers run Yellow Crayon, over on Eucalyptus Street," Syd supplied.

Dolores closed the door in our faces. I shrugged, but it turned out that she was just slipping off the chain. She opened it again.

"Wipe your feet," she said.

We wiped our feet.

"Come on in, then."

We went on in.

You'd expect the house of a mildly crazy person to be messy, wouldn't you? Or the walls to be painted weird colors, or something. But Dolores's house was plain and neat. A red couch sat in front of a small fireplace, and a comfortable-looking armchair sat next to a table piled with books and record albums. Not CDs—records.

Dolores sat on the red couch. Her long gray hair was neatly braided, and she was dressed in blue jeans and a blue denim shirt. I began to relax. She probably wasn't as crazy as people thought.

"So what can I do for you two?" she asked pleasantly. "Got some raffle tickets you want me to buy?"

"No, actually, we came about something else," Syd said. We'd agreed on a cover story before we came. If I'd told Dolores Sakonnet that my real father is a murderer, the whole town would know it in about three seconds.

"Our mothers are planning to hire someone, and we don't trust him," Syd continued. "He lives in another state. Back east. But we think he gave us a fake address and everything."

Dolores leaned forward. "They do that."

"We thought maybe you could tell us how to look up his background and his real address," I said. "We could pay you."

She shook her head. "No need. I'd be

glad to help you. If they hire this man, he'd be moving here, wouldn't he?"

We nodded.

"So what's his name?" Dolores got up and got a pad and pen.

I swallowed. "Silas Murdoch. And he lives somewhere in New England, we think. Maybe Maine."

"You have the address he gave you?" Dolores asked, busily writing.

Syd and I exchanged glances. We hadn't thought that far. Pretty lame of us not to realize that Dolores would ask.

"Thirty-three Pine Street," Syd blurted. "In Portland, Maine."

Dolores wrote it down. "If he's got a criminal record, I'll find out. I'll give you a profile of what he did, and where he went to jail, and if he's on parole." She looked up. "Anything else you want? Credit history?"

"No," I said. "Mainly, we just want to know what he's doing now."

Dolores nodded. "It'll take a day or so. Maybe a little more." She leaned forward, and her milky blue eyes seemed to roll around in her head like marbles. Suddenly, she did look crazy. "You can't be too careful," she said. "Ever."

Syd and I thanked her again, then said we really had to go. We practically ran out of there.

"Do you think we were rude?" Syd asked, eyeing the house.

"Nah. I think it's time for Dolores to beam back up to the mother ship," I said.

I wasn't expecting much, but two days later, Dolores placed a piece of paper in my hand. It told me the charge Silas Murdoch had been convicted of, the number of years he'd served, and where he was living. Bangor, Maine. He worked as a line chef in a seafood restaurant called The Happy Sole. He had an address, but no phone number. It was unlisted.

"I can get it for you," Dolores said. "I know a way. The only thing is, it costs fifty dollars. But if you want—"

"It's okay," I said, staring at the paper. I just wanted to know where Silas was. I didn't want to talk to him.

"I can't believe someone would actually

hire him," Dolores said. "I mean, legally, he has to tell his employer that he did time. Now, you tell your mother not to hire this man."

I was barely listening to her. I was staring at the address of my father.

Suddenly, her hand landed on my arm like a claw.

"Listen to me, Andy," she hissed. "They never go straight. They just pretend to. They wait and they watch, and then they go back to their sneaking, violent ways. Their hearts are black."

Her nails dug into my flesh. Her breath hit me, warm and smelling faintly of onions. "They have no souls!"

I shook off her arm. I stuffed the paper in my back pocket. For the first time since I'd found out the news, I had a tiny bit of sympathy for my father. I had a sense of what he was up against. With people like Dolores, how could any ex-con go straight? What if he was innocent? Nobody would give him a break.

I thanked Dolores and hurried away. As soon as I turned the corner, I stared at the paper again.

My father.

I didn't want to contact him, or talk to him. But at least I had a way to find out more about him.

5//the happy sole

To: happysole@cyber.com
From: ylwcrayon
Subject: employee query

Dear Manager:
Can you contact me at the above address for a personal matter regarding one of your employees?
Thank you.

To: ylwcrayon
From: happysole@cyber.com
Subject: Re: employee query

Be glad to help if I can. What can I do for you?

Bob Treat
Manager, Happy Sole

```
To: happysole@cyber.com
From: ylwcrayon
Subject: background check
```

Dear Mr. Treat:
I work for a company called Yellow
Crayon. Your employee, Silas Murdoch, has
applied to us to fill a part-time position of
freelance consultant. This job would not
require relocation.

However, since our work involves confi-
dential areas of software development, we
need to know that Mr. Murdoch is reliable.
Can you recommend him? We are con-
cerned about his prison record. If you could
add any details, we would appreciate it.
Naturally, this information will remain
confidential, and we hope you will not
inform Mr. Murdoch of our request.

I checked my e-mail every day for Bob
Treat's reply. I felt guilty about the ruse.

What if Bob Treat got angry at Silas for looking for another job behind his back? I said the job was freelance and part-time because I didn't want the manager to think that Silas would be walking off. But you never know what people might think.

When I finally got the e-mail, it was disappointing:

To: ylwcrayon
From: happysole@cyber.com
Subject: Re: background check

Silas Murdoch is a reliable employee. He works hard and is always on time.

Gee, thanks, Mr. Gabby Treat. I'd heard New Englanders didn't talk much, but this was ridiculous.

To: happysole@cyber.com
From: ylwcrayon
Subject: more background

Could you add some details, Mr. Treat? We understand that Mr. Murdoch went to

*prison for manslaughter. Do you feel he has
been rehabilitated?*

```
To: ylwcrayon
From: happysole@cyber.com
Subject: Re: more background
```

*If you want to know more, why don't
you ask Mr. Murdoch?*

Obviously, Mr. Treat had had enough of
snoopy possible employers.

The trail was cold.

But instead of signing off, I did a Web
search of "Famous Trials." I waded through
hundreds of sites, and I just want to report
that there are a scary amount of loonies out
there obsessed with murder.

In the middle of my search, my computer
dinged, meaning someone wanted to talk to
me. I looked up at the little box, expecting
to see Syd's online address: *grossgrrl.* (Not
the most attractive online address, but Syd
claims it keeps away geeks who want a date.
She has enough trouble juggling real dates
to take on cyber ones, she says.) Then I

remembered that I had signed on as ylw-crayon.

It was the Happy Sole. Maybe Bob Treat had changed his mind!

But these words popped up:

This is Silas Murdoch. I never applied for a job at your company, bud, and I don't know who you are. Mind telling me why you're poking around in my business?

It was my dad!

6//family reunion

My fingers shot out toward the "power" button. I felt as if I'd been caught in a crime. As if I were the guilty one.

But I stopped. I told myself that he was three thousand miles away. He couldn't hurt me. He didn't even know who I was.

And here was my chance to get to know just a little bit more about him. I typed out:

I'm a friend of your son's.

It seemed to take forever until the words flashed back.

You know Greg?

My fingers slowly tapped out the response.

His name isn't Greg anymore. It's Andy.

I waited. Sweat broke out on my forehead. I gripped the arms of my chair.

So tell me. He must be fourteen, fifteen now?

Sixteen, I wrote. *He's a junior in high school.*

How's he doing? Is he a smart guy? Does he play football? I can't picture him. The last time I saw the little guy he was sucking on a rattle.

He's an average guy, I wrote. *Pretty good student. Not a bad athlete.*

The words flashed back almost immediately.

Tell me more. Tell me everything.

That's how it started. Soon, Silas and I worked out a routine. We chatted online almost every night. I didn't leave my usual good night message to Syd anymore. I was too busy with Silas.

At first, I just answered questions about myself. Or, I mean, I answered questions about "Andy," as if I were a friend of his, not him. If you know what I mean.

Silas asked me about Andy's grades, and whether he was on any school teams—the guy was a sports nut—and what his new family was like. He seemed totally concerned that Andy didn't have a dad.

I wouldn't have let him get adopted if I knew that. A guy needs a dad.

Even though I was currently not speaking to my mom, I had to admit that she'd done a stellar job of raising me. Sure, I missed having a dad. It's probably the reason I never went in for team sports. Way back in Little League, I just couldn't stand having the other dads come to all the games. I couldn't stand how they cheered, and how after the game, they'd rush over and congratulate the other boys, and tug the brim of their hats down and say, *Way to go.*

Mom tried. She came to the games and she actually knows quite a bit about baseball. She did all the right things. She cheered, but not too loudly, so she wouldn't embarrass me. She played catch with me and taught me how to bat. She's an awesome softball player. There was just one problem.

She wasn't a dad.

So I dropped out of team sports. I like to shoot hoops with Syd, and I've played coed softball a million times with friends in the park. But I never went out for football, or even track.

When Silas said that—*A guy needs a dad*—I didn't respond. But something in my heart twisted. I knew he wanted to be a dad. Wished he had been a dad.

One night, Silas wrote about me as a baby.

I'm surprised Andy didn't grow up to be a jock. When he was a baby, I named him Rocket. He had some pitching arm. He was always throwing stuff out of his crib.

I nearly fell off my chair. Rocket! It was my e-mail address! I had made up a Yellow Crayon address, just to put more distance between us. There was no way that Silas could know that I'd picked Rocket Man as my address.

Which is so weird, it's scary. I'd picked it because I've always liked that old Elton John song: "It's lonely out in space . . . " I'd felt that way sometimes. As if I were drifting in a big, black universe.

Could it be that somehow I'd remembered my dad calling me Rocket? Was that why I'd felt a chill the first time I'd heard the song?

What a total, exceptional spook-out.

That night, I wondered if my connection to my father might be deeper than I knew. Syd would call it "cosmic."

All I knew was that something tugged at me. Something ran between us. Deeper than I'd imagined. Deeper than any explanation.

Deeper than any crime. . . .

You haven't asked me about my prison sentence. I know you know about it. Does Andy know?

He knows. And I didn't like to ask.

And I don't like to talk about it. Because when you say you're innocent, people just say, Sure. Sure you are.

But I didn't feel that way anymore. I wanted to know.

I won't say, Sure. *I want to know.*

Okay. Not much to say except I didn't do it. If I'd had money, I'd have hired a good lawyer. And I wasn't thinking clearly, anyway. I was in shock. Pam was dead. My baby was gone. It was like living a nightmare. You just can't focus. You just can't believe it's really happening to you. Then you wake up, and you're in jail.

"Andy?"

I jumped about five feet. Mom had opened my bedroom door.

"It's late," she said. "School tomorrow."

It was after eleven. Which meant that it was after two in the morning back in Maine.

"I'm just about to log off," I said.

She walked a few steps closer, and I panicked. If she saw that I was talking to Silas, who knew what she would do? I shut off the computer. With a *blip*, Silas's words disappeared.

"See?" I said impatiently. "I'm going to bed, okay?"

Mom stopped. I realized that she had walked closer so that she could kiss me good night. Not so she could snoop.

"So good night," I said.

She nodded. "Good night."

The door closed softly. I turned off the lamp so that Mom wouldn't see the light under the door. Then I quickly switched on the computer again. I logged on to my online service and sent a message to Silas.

I didn't mean to cut you off, I wrote. *It was a power surge.*

I thought you didn't believe me. I thought you blew me off. Thought I was full of it.

I don't know what to believe, I wrote.

That's fine. You don't know me. You'd be stupid to believe an ex-con. So would Andy. I shouldn't expect much. That's what I tell myself. Every day.

I didn't write anything. I just waited. I knew that all the way across the country, a man waited, just like I did. Maybe his room was dark, too. His face was in shadow. But maybe the fingers at the keyboard were just like mine.

Then, Silas wrote:

I just wish

He stopped. But he didn't have to finish the sentence. I knew what he felt. I *knew.*

So I wrote:

I lied about being a friend of Andy's. I'm Andy. I'm your son.

Seconds ticked by. The house was quiet.

The blue screen glowed. I felt like Silas and I were the only two people awake in the world.

And then the message flashed back.

I thought so.

I touched the words on the screen and grinned. Was he smiling now, too?

A second later, another message flashed. Just one word.

Hallelujah.

7//grilling

Moms have limits. I guess you know that.

Well, I'd pushed mine to the outer edge of her own personal envelope. On Saturday morning, she opened my bedroom door, stood in the doorway, and took a breath.

"I've apologized. I've given you space. I've tiptoed around you. I've overlooked your rudeness, and I've ignored your hurtful remarks. And I'm done. Finished! I'm still your mother, Andy—*and don't tell me I'm not!*"

I eyed her warily. Mom doesn't lose her temper very often. "I wasn't going to," I said.

"Well, there's a refreshing change," she said, raising an eyebrow. "I invited Rachel and Syd for dinner tonight. It's time this household at least went through the motions of normality. Okay?"

"Okay," I said.

She still stood there, as if she was waiting for me to tell her I wouldn't be there, or I'd stay in my room.

"Mom," I said gently. "I said okay."

She looked lost for a moment. "Okay," she said, and shut the door.

Syd's mom is a vegetarian, so we were having grilled swordfish. Syd is a vegetarian, too, except for cheeseburgers.

Mom made these roasted potatoes with garlic that I can eat by the truckful, and Syd's favorite dessert, this awesome apple crumble with vanilla ice cream. Obviously, she was trying to please.

Mom got the barbecue grill fired up, and Rachel wandered into the kitchen to make the salad dressing. It's the only thing we let Rachel make. She is an awful cook. But if you ever want to know a hundred things you can make with soybeans, Rachel Gross is your man.

I sat on the lawn, away from the smoke

of the barbecue. Everything seemed totally back to normal, except that everything was totally different. Life can be funny that way. It's weird how your life can be blown to bits, and you can be holding this awful secret, and you keep on having to go to barbecues.

Syd came over and sat next to me on the grass. She was wearing frayed denim shorts and hiking boots with no socks. Not exactly a fashion plate.

"Hey, Beanhead," she said. I should mention that Syd has called me Beanhead since the seventh grade, when I ate four helpings of my mom's three-bean salad at a picnic. Now she calls me that because she claims that my brain is the size of a bean. "But that's okay," she says. "All sixteen-year-old guys have brains the size of a bean."

"Kidney or navy?" I'd said.

Now, Syd leaned back on her elbows and crossed her ankles. "I've got news for you. This is a barbecue, not a funeral."

"And so. . . ."

She nudged me with her shoulder. "Can't

you lighten up? I gave up a Saturday night date for this."

"With who?"

"Jamie Tulver." Syd squinted at me. "And Jamie is currently my number one favorite date."

"Are you ranking them now?" I grumbled. Okay, maybe in my description of Syd I made her sound like a tomboy type. She is. But she is also a killer. She lines up guys like bowling pins and knocks them down without breaking a sweat.

"Nah," Syd said. She grunted as she untied her hiking boots. "I give him an A for effort, though." Syd slipped off her boots and wiggled her little pink toes in the grass. "What about you, Andy? You haven't mentioned Silas in a while. Wait." Syd put a finger to her temple. "As a matter of fact, you've been avoiding me."

"I have not," I said.

Syd didn't answer. Did I mention that she doesn't acknowledge a lie? She just lets it hang there in the air, echoing, so you feel like a prize jerk.

I looked up at my house. It was built as a

small summer cottage back in the nineteen thirties. Someone had enclosed the back porch, which is all paned windows. The house is pretty cozy, but it's basically a mess.

"Have you noticed that our house needs a paint job?" I asked Syd.

"Don't change the subject," she said.

"I'm not," I said. "It probably needs a new roof, too. Every time it rains, there's a puddle in the kitchen. The screen door really squeaks. It's squeaked for years. And the car keeps breaking down because Mom forgets to do things like change the oil."

Syd got it. She always gets it. She fixed me with her smoke-gray eyes. Her eyebrows swooped down like raven wings as she glowered at me. "What are you telling me, Andy? That your car and your house would be perfect if you had a *dad*?"

I shrugged.

"Yeah, Beanhead," Syd snorted. "And you'd have a football scholarship to Notre Dame."

"All I'm saying—" I started.

"I know what you're saying, and you'd

better rethink it," Syd interrupted, her eyes flashing. "First of all, it's completely sexist—"

"Wait a sec—"

"Where are you living, in TV world?" Syd said. "Not all dads are handymen. Have you noticed that my very own mom can fix the plumbing and rewire a lamp with one hand tied behind her back? And second of all, it's stupid. Practically everybody is born with something they have to get over. Take me." Syd smirked. "Sydney Gross. I've got the name of some eighty-year-old guy with halitosis and sock garters ranting about the price of pot roast. Try that on for size."

"That's so close to my situation," I said. "Thanks for the help. All I'm saying is that I'm starting to realize that there are things missing in my life, okay?"

"There are things missing in *everybody's* life," Syd said. "My parents are divorced. My grandparents died in a car crash because some jerk drank three six-packs one night and decided to drive to the 7-Eleven for a Milky Way. Grow up."

"Your sympathy is so touching," I said. I was truly sore at Syd. First she blamed me for not talking to her. But when I did, she blasted me into smithereens. I ask you—is that fair?

"Oh, darn!" Mom cried.

Syd and I stopped glaring at each other and looked over at Wendy.

"I forgot to make the mango salsa for the swordfish," Mom called across the lawn to us. "I bought all the ingredients, too. I have such a beautiful mango!"

"Relax, Mom," I said. Mom looked as though she were about to bust a gut over a fruit. But I knew she'd wanted the dinner to be perfect.

"It's not too late, Wendy," Rachel said. "You haven't even put the fish on. We can chop up salsa in a jiffy."

"I saw the recipe on the food channel, and it would be perfect," Mom said.

Mom's major form of relaxation is watching the cable food channel and reading cooking magazines at the same time. She gets this totally zonked look on her face, and if I happen to be in the room, I hear her murmur Martian-type things like, *Oooh—ceviche*, or, *Gravlax!*

At the end of the week, the channel posts all the recipes on their Web page. I usually download a bunch of them for Mom. It's our Friday ritual.

Mom looked across the lawn at me. I knew she was wondering if I'd done it this week. And the funny thing was, I had. I *almost* hadn't done it.

"I downloaded the recipes," I told her. "They're probably still in my printer."

"Why don't you get the recipe?" Rachel suggested. "We can chop everything out here. It's such a beautiful evening."

"Great idea, Rach," Mom said. She hurried into the house.

"Now, where were we?" I said to Syd.

"You were just about to admit that you are an idiot," Syd said.

"Was not," I said. "I was about to forgive you for not being understanding and sympathetic and warm, like most girls."

"There you go again, being sexist," Syd said. "You're such a caveman."

"Just let me get my club," I said. I felt relieved. It might look like we were still arguing. But this was standard operating conversation for Syd and me.

Rachel brought out a bowl of tortilla chips and set them on the outdoor table along with mangoes and the rest of the salsa ingredients.

"Food at last," I said, standing up. This dinner was going to turn out okay. I realized why Mom had asked Rachel and Syd over, and why Syd had canceled a date to come. I did feel better. I felt at home again, if that makes any sense.

But suddenly, I realized that Mom had been gone for minutes longer than she had to.

And I remembered that last night, I had printed out all my e-mails to Silas, and his replies. They were in my printer, too.

Mom isn't a snoop. But she wouldn't be able to ignore what was right in front of her eyes.

Syd pushed the tortilla chips toward me. "Eat." She peered at me. "Andy?"

The squeak of the screen door made me look up. Mom stood in the doorway. Her hands were full of papers.

"That's some recipe," Syd said.

Mom's gaze blazed across the patio. "Are

you writing to this man?" she demanded. She held the fistful of papers out toward me and shook them. "Are you?"

At Mom's tone, Syd and Rachel both whipped their heads around and stared at me.

"He's not *that man*," I said. "He's my father!"

"You don't have a father!" Mom shouted. "He gave up that right when he killed your mother!"

"We don't know that for sure," I said. The words sounded good out loud. They'd been in my head for so long. We *didn't* know it for sure. And how could the guy on the Net, the guy who wanted to know me, who remembered tiny details of my baby-hood, who *missed* what he'd had, have destroyed it in such a bloody, horrible way?

Mom grew even more pale. I saw her swallow. "Are you telling me," she said slowly, "that this man has convinced you that he's innocent?"

"I just said I have doubts," I said. "That I don't know for sure. You're not listening to me, as usual."

Mom crumpled the papers in her fist. "This man," she said, thrusting her fist toward me, "took an eight-inch knife and *stabbed* a woman repeatedly until she was *dead*. Then he *lied* about it—"

"You don't know that!" I shouted. "You don't know anything! You just know what you read in the papers!"

Syd and Rachel's heads swiveled back and forth, as if they were in a tennis match.

"Andy, don't you realize you're better off not knowing him?" Mom pleaded. "Don't you realize how he could wreck your life? If he knows where you live—"

"Well, he doesn't," I said. "I didn't tell him. We just talk, okay? It's perfectly innocent—"

"Innocent? This man isn't *innocent,*" Mom said bitterly. "He *stabbed* your poor mother to death—"

"Stop it!" I screamed. I banged my fist on the table. "Stop it!"

Rachel stepped forward. She held up a hand. "Okay," she said quietly. "Okay. Time out. Let's just all take a breath."

Mom and I didn't look at each other. Syd

stared at us, wide-eyed. She'd never seen either of us shout before, I guess. The emotion on the patio was like a black cloud, smothering us. It was hard to breathe.

Rachel slipped off the elastic band that held her curly dark hair back. Then she refastened it. It's a habit she has when she's collecting her thoughts. "Maybe we can find some common ground here."

"Common ground?" Mom said. "I don't think so."

"Wendy, honey, hold on," Rachel said.

Rachel and Mom have been partners for a long time. Mom is the excitable one. She yells at late suppliers, people who overcharge. She gets upset when they lose contracts. Rachel is the one who smoothes clients' feelings and takes them out to lunch. She is calm and logical, like Syd. Mom has this habit of hooking up with the wrong men, too. We call them Bad Boyfriends. It's Rachel who counsels her, puts the pieces back together, points out to Mom when she is making the same mistake, over and over again. Thanks to Rachel, Mom hasn't had a Bad Boyfriend in three years.

Rachel held her gaze until Mom took a deep breath. "Okay," Mom said.

"Wendy, as long as Andy's contact is on the Internet, he can't come to any harm," Rachel said. "The man doesn't know where he lives, after all. Right?"

"There's psychic harm, Rachel," Mom said steadily. "There's emotional damage."

Rachel nodded. "I know," she said gently. She turned to me. "Andy, you can understand why your mom is concerned, can't you? She wants to protect you. And this man did do time"—She held up a hand when I started to protest—"You know the term 'reasonable doubt,' don't you? This jury didn't have a reasonable doubt. They thought he was guilty."

"Are you telling me that every person in jail is guilty?" I asked.

"No," Rachel said. "But this man could be guilty. And if he is—"

"I wish you two would call him by his name," I said. "Silas."

Mom shuddered.

"I think the question is, *why* are you pursuing this relationship?" Rachel asked me. "And what are the reasons that you think he's innocent?"

Rachel fixed me with the honest gaze that was so much like Syd's. I knew she wanted an answer. I mean a real answer, one that told her what was in my heart and on my mind.

But I didn't have a good answer, I realized. At least, not one that would convince Rachel or Syd or my mom.

Why did I think he could be innocent? Because I felt it in my gut. I just knew it.

But I couldn't tell them that. The Moms would trade this knowing, superior glance. And Rachel would talk to me in therapy-speak about my father fixation. Syd would join in.

Who needed it?

"Hey, who's getting grilled here?" I said finally. "Me, or the swordfish?"

"Andy," Mom said quietly, "I want you to really think about this. You could be putting us all in danger. What if he comes here?"

"He doesn't know where I live, okay?" I said. "I didn't tell him."

"How did you find him, Andy?" Rachel asked curiously. "It couldn't have been easy." Now that was a question I didn't particularly want to answer. But I gave them a quick version of what happened.

"Wait a second," Mom said slowly. "You used the name of our company? He could look that up! He could find you!"

"He wouldn't go to all that trouble," I said. "It's hard to find someone through an e-mail address."

"Andy, we have a Web site," Mom said. "And it lists our address. It would be very easy for him to do that."

Oops.

"Look, he doesn't even know my last name," I said. "He doesn't want to intrude on my life. He said he wouldn't try to contact me in person until I was ready—"

"Until you're *ready?*" Mom yelled, her face flushed. She was angry all over again. "Are you telling me you'd actually want to meet this madman?"

"The madman is my *dad!*" I shouted back. "And what are you? You're not innocent. You've lied to me my whole life!

At least my father tells the truth!"

Mom shook her head angrily. It was a standoff.

We stood across the patio from each other. But we might have been miles and miles away from each other.

I realized right then that I'd started down a new path. I couldn't turn back. It was almost as though I'd chosen Silas over my mom.

But I couldn't help it. I wanted to tell her that. I wanted to tell her that finding Silas had been like taking a long drink of cool water. I wanted to say that it was like filling a hole you hadn't known was there.

So I had to keep going. No matter what. No matter who got hurt.

8//the madman is my dad

Mom must have seen in my eyes how I was feeling. She started to cry and ran into the house. Rachel followed her.

So much for mango salsa.

Syd looked at me. She lifted one eyebrow. "Cheeseburger?"

Syd squirted mustard on her French fries. She spooned relish on her cheeseburger. We'd driven into town and stopped at the Red Bird Café, our favorite place to hang.

"Double whammy," she said, taking a big bite. She chewed and swallowed. "Not only am I eating meat, I'm eating dairy. Mom would totally plotz."

"Dairy?"

"It's her new thing," Syd said. "She wants

us to give up dairy. Calls it 'moo glue.' Have you ever tasted soy milk?" Syd took a bite of her pickle. "Talk about *glue*."

She swirled a French fry in mustard and ate it. She watched me push my cheeseburger around my plate and took another bite of hers.

"Emotional trauma makes me hungry," she said.

"Everything makes you hungry," I said.

Syd nodded, agreeing. "I've never seen you and Wendy go at it like that before. Do you hate her, or what?"

"I don't hate her," I said.

"Well, you sure sounded like you do," Syd said.

"I hate what she did," I said. "I hate that she lied to me."

"Andy, I have a piece of advice for you." Syd pointed a French fry at me. "Get over it. Because you've got other problems. Like, why are you treating a homicidal maniac like dear old dad?"

I pushed away my plate and started to rise. "I don't need this."

"Calm down." Syd put a hand on my arm. "Let's just talk, okay?"

I sat down and stared at my plate. Syd peered at me. "Still mad?"

"You bet."

Syd bit her lip worriedly. "Because of what I said?"

"No," I said. "Because you got mustard on my sleeve."

Syd laughed. She stuck her napkin in her glass of water, then crossed to my side of the booth. She started dabbing at the stain on my sleeve.

"I'll make a deal with you," she said. "I'll stop with the smart-aleck remarks if you'll really talk to me. Deal?"

"Deal," I said.

She looked up. Our faces were really close. When she blinked, I noticed how thick and dark Syd's eyelashes are. Her eyes are such an unusual color. A darker color runs around the iris. They are the prettiest eyes.

I must have looked weird, because Syd backed up fast, as though I were about to bite her. She slid back into her side of the booth and picked up her cheeseburger.

"So talk to me, Beanhead," she said.

"I know your parents are divorced," I told Syd. "But your dad lives in the next town, and you see him all the time. He's a part of your life. A really important part. Can you imagine turning your back on him?"

Syd hesitated. "It's just not the same, Andy—"

"I know it isn't the same," I said. "But it's still about fathers. It's still about that connection, right?"

Syd took a huge bite of cheeseburger and nodded. I think she took the bite so that she wouldn't have to comment.

"I've been talking to him for a while now," I went on. "He's really careful not to push. But I know he's really happy to have me back in his life. He remembers me as a baby, Syd. He remembers what I liked to eat, what made me laugh, the games he used to play with me . . . does that sound like a cold-blooded killer?"

Syd shrugged and ate a fry.

"What if he's not lying?" I said. "What if he really is innocent? Don't I owe him something? He's my father. We should have been in each other's lives. I could have had a totally different life, Syd!"

Syd put down her burger. Shaking her head, she wiped her mouth with a napkin. "On a cosmic level, everything happens the way it should," she said. "Wendy is the mom you *should* have. Don't confuse the issues."

I hate when Syd sounds like a cosmic goon. "Does that mean my real mom was meant to be murdered?" I asked, annoyed.

"Of course not," Syd snapped. But she stopped and sighed. "Okay. Let's break down the situation. You think your dad could be innocent, so you want to give him a chance, right?"

"Right," I said.

"Let me ask you this." Syd's eyes narrowed. "If he is guilty—I'm saying if, okay?—will you still want him in your life?"

"Of course not," I said.

"So that leaves an obvious course of action," Syd said. "First, you continue the relationship, but only through the Net. That protects you. Second, you do more research into the trial."

"More research?" I asked. "What will that get me?"

"Maybe you could find something," Syd said, pushing her plate away. "Who knows? Your dad probably didn't have a great lawyer, right?"

"He said he was the worst."

"Well, maybe something was overlooked. Maybe you could find a way to prove him innocent. What about DNA testing? Or some clue that was missed back then?" Syd leaned forward. "Just think, Andy. You could clear your dad!"

Mom's door was closed when I got home. The kitchen was clean, and the grill rolled back to its usual position under the eave of the garage.

There was a note on my pillow.

Andy,

I'm sorry about before. I lost my temper. This situation is difficult for everyone concerned, and the best we can do is try not to hurt each other.

I've taken a hot bath, and I'm going to hit the sack. Let's talk tomorrow.

And remember, I love you.
Mom

I folded the note and put it in my sock drawer. The next time I got angry at Mom, I'd look at it. She was right—as usual. I should try harder not to hurt her.

I hate when she's right.

I turned on the computer. There was an e-mail from Silas telling me that he'd log on at eleven P.M., my time, if I wanted to talk.

It was ten to eleven. I wasn't sure if I wanted to talk to him tonight. I was pretty beat. But as I hesitated, the "instant message" box blinked on. I couldn't ignore it.

Hey, Andy. How's it hangin?

I was just about to go to bed, I tapped out.

Bad day?

Had better, I wrote. I was about to sign off, but Silas's message popped up quickly.

Tell me about it.

It's Mom. She found out I'd made contact with you. I guess she went a little ballistic.

Makes sense, Silas replied. *In her eyes,*

I'm not what you'd call a model dad. She doesn't know me.

If she did, she probably wouldn't be as freaked, I replied. Silas was pretty understanding, considering. More understanding than Mom was!

Give her time. Sooner or later she'll figure out I'm not the big bad wolf.

Definitely later, I wrote.

Mom and I never had that talk the next day. She made these awesome Western omelettes for breakfast, and our peace felt pretty fragile. I guess we both decided to let the whole thing slide for a few days.

The few days turned into a week. We had our midsemester break at school. The rich kids headed to the Sierras to ski, and the not-so-rich kids, like me, bummed around home.

Mom had wanted to start a garden for about a hundred years. I decided on the first Saturday of vacation that it might make a pretty good peacemaking project to at least start it. Besides, Mom was spending all day at the office. There was a dirt patch in back that Mom had worked on last year, before she got too busy at work. But once I went out to look at it, I realized that the whole yard needed a little pick-me-up first. The grass needed cutting, and the hedges needed trimming.

It was a chore, but I felt okay about doing it. I didn't mind the exercise, and Mom would be super grateful. Plus, it was one of those freakish warm February days you can get in California. The sun was pouring down like gold, and the sky was clear blue and empty of clouds.

Mom has an old-fashioned mower, one that doesn't have a motor. She says she doesn't want to add to pollution, and besides, she needs the exercise. But the thing is a pain to push around, so the result is that we put off mowing the lawn for as long as we can.

I started on the front lawn. But I got hot, and stopped in the middle. I had a feeling it would not improve our mother-and-child relations if I left the lawn half mowed.

I sat on the porch step to rest. I watched a man in jeans walk down the block, moving from dappled shade to sunlight as he passed under the trees. His hair was short and sandy, and the sun glinted off the blond strands.

He stopped at the end of the walk. I wondered if he was selling something, or looking for work. There was something about his face that told me he'd lived a hard life. He was handsome, though, muscular and strong. Even from the porch steps, I could see that his eyes were a pale color. Green, like mine.

And then I knew.

I stood up. He smiled, and lines radiated out from around his eyes. "Andy?"

I gulped. "Dad?"

9//nuclear blast family

He didn't move forward. And I didn't think I could move forward. Or back. I was stuck in the moment.

"I guess I blew it," he said ruefully. "I debated about whether or not to call. Then I thought, maybe if I just walk by, I'll catch a glimpse of him. But when I saw you, I had to stop."

"Why are you here?" I asked. My voice sounded like our creaking screen door.

"Can I—" he gestured at the walk that led to the house "—hard to talk from a distance, isn't it? But I'd understand if you didn't want me on the property."

"No, no," I said quickly. "You can come in."

As he moved toward me I realized he

wasn't tall. He just gave that impression. I was actually taller than he was.

He stood in front of me. A slow smile spread over his face. "How do you like that. I'm shorter than my kid."

"Silas," I said, "what are you doing here?"

"You asked me to come," he said. "It just took me a little time to wrap things up back in Maine. I knew that you were upset about your mother not accepting me. You said that if she knew me, she'd come around. So here I am."

He looked up at the house, and at the half-mowed lawn. "Nice place," he said.

I felt really stupid. I hadn't asked Silas to come. It hadn't even been in my mind when I'd said that about Mom. But I couldn't exactly ask him to leave, either.

"Don't worry," he said suddenly. I realized he had stopped looking at the house and was watching me. "I'm not staying. I'm on my way to Seattle. Got a buddy up there I haven't seen in years."

"It's just that—" *Mom is going to freak. I don't really know you. Just looking at you, hearing you talk, makes me feel completely spacey.*

"Yeah," he said softly. "It's weird, isn't it?"

It was weirder than weird. I stared at him, a stranger to me, and tried to find something that was familiar. His hands and feet were broad, and mine were long and skinny.

"You've got your mother's feet," he said.

Our features weren't alike. You'd never pick us out in a crowd as father and son. Except for his eyes.

"At least you've got green eyes, like me," Silas said. "But you take after your mother. She was tall and skinny, like you."

"She was?"

"Real pretty," Silas said.

"Do you have a picture of her?" I blurted.

Silas looked away. "I don't have any pictures. I don't have anything left from that life. Just memories. I kind of like it better, in a way. Memories are good things."

"You have good memories?"

"I've got a million and one good memories, kid," he said softly. Then he grinned.

"So tell me. Where did you get a name like Andy? Sounds like a wimp. That's what you get when you let a woman pick a name. I named you Greg. Now, there's a man's name."

The sun went behind a cloud, and shadows fell on the lawn. A breeze scampered across my skin, cooling the perspiration and making me shiver. Suddenly, I wasn't sure about the person standing in front of me. Had I been crazy to think he was innocent? He looked hardened and strong, not the broken man I'd pictured, the one I was starting to feel sorry for. I couldn't imagine anyone feeling sorry for Silas Murdoch. There was something intimidating about him. Something almost . . . scary.

But then his eyes twinkled at me, as if we were sharing a huge joke. "Just kidding. Look at your face! Hey, you Californians are laid back, right? But I know my kid's not a wimp."

"I'm no wimp," I said. I hesitated. "Just a wussy coward."

Silas threw back his head and roared with laughter. I laughed, too. And suddenly, everything felt completely comfortable.

"You said you wound up things in Maine," I said. "Does that mean that you left for good?"

He nodded. "I didn't have a choice. Lost my job and couldn't find another one."

"You got fired?"

He shrugged. "The boss didn't like hearing about my prison years. I know, I know, I should have told him. But I needed a job."

It was my fault, then. I'd told Bob Treat about his record.

"Hey, wipe that guilty expression off your face, kid," Silas said. "It wasn't your fault. And it was time to move on. Since being in prison, I get antsy if I stay in one place too long. Speaking of which, do you know of a cheap motel nearby? I left my bag at the bus station."

"Sure. There's a motel on the highway, right near the station," I said. "I'll drive you there."

He looked over at the lawn. "Looks like I interrupted a chore. Why don't we get this done first? You shouldn't leave a chore half done."

"That's okay," I said. "Let me get the keys."

I ran inside the house and snatched up my wallet and car keys. I wondered what to do after I dropped off Silas. Should I invite him for dinner? I wanted to. Mom would pass out, then wake up and pass out again.

But if Silas was here, and I wanted to see him, she really had no choice.

I hit the front porch. Silas had rolled the mower closer to the house.

"You ready, son?"

Son. That sounded totally exceptional.

"Ready," I said.

After I dropped Silas off at the motel, I drove straight to Mom's office. When it comes to tough stuff, it's better to get it over with. That's my motto.

Besides, I'd asked Silas to dinner.

The Moms were in the middle of a pretty heavy discussion when I arrived. They were both wearing these very serious expressions that meant I was a major interruption.

Not the best timing. But I asked if I could talk to Mom alone.

"Sure, sweetie," Mom said.

"I'll get some tea. Want anything, Andy?" Rachel asked.

I shook my head. Mom led me into her office and closed the door. She perched on the edge of her desk. "What's up?"

I hesitated. All of a sudden, it didn't seem such an easy thing to tell her.

She sighed. "Is this about Silas?"

I nodded. I swallowed. "He's here."

She shot off her desk. "He's what?"

"Not *here*. Not in your office," I said quickly. "He's in Verona."

She didn't say anything. She didn't move.

"I asked him to dinner," I said. My voice came out defiantly, as if I were daring her to argue. "I want to get to know him, Mom," I added.

Mom looked at the floor, and I watched her breathe for several too-long seconds.

"You said he wouldn't just show up," she said finally.

I shifted my feet. "Well, there was this kind of misunderstanding," I explained. "He thought I kind of asked him to come. And in a way, I guess I kind of did."

I waited for Mom to nail me on the most lame-o sentence I've ever uttered in my entire life (and that's saying something). But she didn't.

"I guess I'd rather you see him in the safety of your own home," she said slowly. She looked up at me. "Is he staying long?"

I shook my head. "He said he'd be taking off soon. He just wanted to see me, I guess. So, is it okay that I asked him to dinner?"

Mom let out a long breath. "I'll make chicken," she said.

Then she nailed me with her blue crystal gaze. "But I won't fuss."

Silas didn't bring flowers. That was his first smart move. He brought this enormous bouquet of herbs—fresh basil, parsley, mint, rosemary. I could see that if it had been anybody else bringing her bunches of fresh herbs, Mom would have caved right there. But she just took them without a smile.

"I'll put these away," she said shortly. She didn't even say thanks.

Things stayed at that general frosty level for quite a while. We made stilted conversation in the living room. We talked about the weather, and the differences between Maine and California. Riveting stuff. Then Mom went in to check the chicken she was roasting. She'd forgotten to turn the oven on.

"Let me help," Silas said, springing up.

Mom turned frosty. "I can make something else." She turned to go back into the kitchen.

Silas followed her, anyway. I trailed behind, wondering what he was up to. Mom was just taking down a package of pasta from the shelf.

"Really," she said, exasperated when Silas walked in. "I don't need any help."

"But I'd really like to," Silas said, so quietly and politely that it was hard for her to resist. "Let me cut up the chicken," he went on. "I'll fillet the breasts and pound them, and we can sauté them in a little olive oil, lemon, and herbs."

"I can do that," Mom said. She was still annoyed.

"But why should you?" Silas nodded at the pasta box. "You can make the pasta."

So, amazingly enough, Silas and Mom worked side by side in the kitchen, collaborating on the meal. We had lemon chicken and pasta with the herbs Silas had brought, along with sliced fresh tomatoes with basil.

The most amazing part of the meal was once the conversation really got going. It turned out that Silas and Mom had lots of things in common. And not just general things, like they both liked to cook. They both had this major jones for Italy. And not just Italy, but this certain region in Italy. They both wanted to visit the same town.

Then it turned out that in his spare time, Silas liked to hike in the mountains. Mom is a fiend for hiking. And his dream vacation—if he couldn't go to that hillside Italian town—would be Lake Louise, in Canada. Mom has been talking about taking a trip to Lake Louise for years.

Syd would say that Silas and Mom had known each other in a past life. I had gone from being glad they were getting along to feeling a little left out. But I didn't mind. Not at all.

Mom got this dazed expression on her

face, as though every once in a while she was saying to herself, *I actually have a lot in common with a murderer.* Nobody was more surprised than I was.

She hadn't melted completely. But she was definitely softer. Then Silas insisted on doing the dishes.

"You work hard enough," he told Mom. "Why don't you relax with Andy? But first, can I have a word with you?"

"I'll clear the dishes," I said, jumping up. I stacked them quickly and took them into the kitchen. But I stayed by the swinging door, my ear plastered to the crack.

"I know this evening is about the last thing you wanted to do," Silas said quietly. I had to strain to catch the words. "First, I want to thank you for your hospitality."

"It meant a lot to Andy," Mom said.

"Second of all—and I know there's no reason in the world for you to believe this— I want to tell you that I didn't kill my wife. I know—why am I bothering to say it, when you won't believe me? I guess I just need to. For me. I find that when I meet someone I respect, I can't stop myself from saying the words out loud. So here it is, Wendy. I loved my wife. I didn't kill her. Losing her and my son was the single worst thing that has happened to me. It changed me forever. But it changed me for the *better*. Because maybe I didn't appreciate enough what I had."

"You don't have to—" Mom murmured, but Silas must have stopped her.

"Now God has given me a second chance here. I've seen my son. I've had a couple of laughs with him. A meal. What I'm hungry for is more of it. But I want you to know, if you think he'll be better off without me in his life, I'm gone. Tonight. I'm not leaving it up to Andy. Or me. You're the one who can see clearest and best, out of all of us. So tell me, ma'am. Is it better that I go?"

I pressed against the door frame. I held my breath. I waited, counting the seconds.

One, two, three, four . . .

Mom's voice was just a murmur. "Stay."

10//day by day

Wendy wasn't won over—not by a long shot. And, may I point out, neither was I. We were both taking it day by day. Sometimes, that's all you can do.

I told Silas about my plan to start on Mom's vegetable garden, and he insisted on helping. "I want to do something for you before I leave," he told me.

We went to the nursery together and bought the tools we'd need, and investigated how to create the best topsoil without chemicals. Later, we'd buy tomato plants and herbs.

Then we started on the back plot. We worked side by side, sweating and digging. We didn't even talk much. Silas liked to whistle. And I liked to listen to it.

Silas usually met me at the house after Mom had gone to work. But on Tuesday, I decided to save him the walk. We only have one car, but sometimes, if Mom has time, she walks to work.

I drove to the motel and asked at the desk for him. That's when I found out he wasn't registered. He'd checked out last Sunday, after staying only one night.

I drove back home slowly. Silas had lied to me. I didn't like the feeling. Something sour had trickled into our relationship. It wasn't a big lie. But it was surprising how much it hurt.

Then I told myself not to jump to conclusions. There could be plenty of reasons he wasn't staying at the motel. He'd found someplace cheaper. He couldn't stand the noise of the highway. He wanted room service.

He walked up at 9:15, right on time. I was waiting outside on the front stoop.

"What a morning!" he called as he came toward me. "Back in Maine, they're probably shoveling through three feet of snow. Here I am, strolling through daisies."

I stood up. "You walked from the motel?"

"I always walk from the motel." Silas eyed me. "What is it, Rocket?"

"I went there to pick you up," I said. "You're not registered. As a matter of fact, you checked out two days ago."

His gaze slid away from mine. He studied the lawn for a moment. "I've been sleeping outside, Andy. In the park. I didn't want to tell you."

"But, why?"

His mouth twisted bitterly. "Why do you think people sleep outside, kid? Because they like it?"

"You don't have money."

"Bingo."

"I guess I just thought—"

"Yeah." Silas nodded. "It's okay. I let you think it. But, hey, don't worry about it. I'm looking for a job—got to make enough money to get on the road to Seattle, set myself up there. So don't worry about me."

"You can move in here," I blurted.

"No, Rocket." He gave a small, twisted smile. "Your mom would never go for it."

"There's an apartment over the garage," I said. "Mom and Rachel used to have their office there, before they moved to town. There's a pullout couch."

He shook his head.

"I'll ask her," I said. "You can't sleep outside, Silas!"

"Okay, okay," he said. "You can ask her. But no pressure!"

"No pressure," I agreed.

"You've got to do it," I told Mom. "He's sleeping in the park!"

"That's his choice, Andy," Mom said. "He's the one who came cross-country without money. He's *expecting* you to ask him to stay. He's manipulating you. Can't you see it?"

"He didn't tell me he was sleeping in the park," I told her. "I found out. He didn't want me to know."

Mom creased her paper napkin. She had already folded it into a tiny square. We'd gone out for one of our favorite dinners, hot dogs with everything at Susy's Barking Dog.

"I don't want him on our property, Andy," she said quietly.

"You're jealous of him," I said. "You can't stand the fact that I want to get to know him! You'll keep me apart from him how ever you can. Just because you're not my real mother!"

Mom's face tightened. She crumpled up the napkin and stuffed it into her empty drink cup.

"Fine. Let him stay there," she said. "Two weeks, Andy. That's it!"

That's it," I promised.

Now that Silas was staying in the garage apartment, he came over for breakfast every morning. Actually, he made it. He sliced fresh fruit for my mom, and made pancakes or eggs for me.

Since Mom wasn't charging him any rent, Silas insisted on fixing things up around the house. He had been a carpenter before he'd gone to jail, and we have a complete tool set from when Mom had decided she was going to fix everything that went wrong in the house.

Um, would it surprise you to know that she never did?

But Silas strapped on the old tool belt and fixed the shelves in the pantry, shaved the door that always stuck, and even built bookshelves for Mom's home office.

I knew that even though Mom wasn't crazy about having Silas around, she couldn't help appreciating what he did. All those little things that drove us nuts were finally fixed.

Okay. Let me stop right here. I'm not a complete idiot. I know that Silas was probably helping out so that he could get on my good side. And I hadn't forgotten, not for a minute, that he could have killed someone. Could have killed my birth mother.

But at night, when I'd lie in bed, with the windows opened and the breeze drifting against my skin, I'd know Mom was in the next room with the light on, and Silas was near, and I would feel something good, something real. I would feel safe. Like I was in a family for the very first time.

Syd came by Friday morning when Silas and I were working in the garden. We'd planned to buy some tomato plants that afternoon and start planting.

Syd stood, her hands in her pockets, her legs spread. The posture seemed a tad . . . aggressive?

Maybe she was just the tiniest bit upset that I hadn't called or come by since Silas had arrived. And our usual nightly e-mail habit had been shelved for the duration.

"Syd!" I said. I put down the shovel. "Hey!" I sounded just a little too chipper.

"Hey, yourself," Syd said. She looked right past me, right at Silas.

He wiped his hand on his jeans. "Well, now. You'd better introduce me to this pretty thing, Andy. I've heard that California girls are the prettiest in the country, and I've been waiting for proof."

Syd's expression was completely neutral. "You must be Andy's birth father. I heard you were visiting."

"Silas Murdoch." Silas held out his hand, and Syd shook it reluctantly.

"Mr. Murdoch—"

He grinned at her. "Silas. I'm not *that* old."

"Mr. Murdoch," Syd said, "would you

mind if I borrow Andy for a second? I need to talk to him."

"You go right ahead," Silas said. He leaned toward me. "Uh-oh. Watch your back, Rocket. I have a feeling you're in the doghouse."

I followed Syd uneasily across the lawn. As soon as we were out of earshot, she turned to me.

But I didn't give her the chance to speak first. "Okay, I know," I said. "I've been ignoring you, right? I should have come by."

"Why is that, Andy?" Syd asked mildly. "Because for months we'd planned all the things we'd do on our school break? Because we were supposed to take the bus to San Francisco for the day? Because we were going to have a picnic on Angel Island? Because—"

"I thought you'd be busy with Jamie Tulver or one of the other million guys you date," I said. I knew it was lame. Syd never lets her active dating life come between us.

Syd squinted at me. "What's happened to

you? Are you taking jerk lessons from that macho lunkhead?"

"Hey!" I said. "That's my father!"

"He's not your father, Andy," Syd said in a harsh whisper. "He's a stranger. Don't forget that."

"Here we go," I said. "It's your 'She Who Must Be Obeyed' act. You just met him! Why can't you give him a chance? I know he didn't exactly come off great, okay? He was just trying to impress you."

Syd's face was grim. "It didn't work."

"He's been in prison for over ten years," I said. "Maybe his manners aren't the greatest."

"Would you listen to yourself?" Syd said. "You keep giving this lame knee-jerk defense of him."

"It's not knee-jerk," I said. "I've gotten to know him. Silas is totally into doing this project for Mom. You know she's been talking about having a vegetable garden for ages. I think it's a really nice gesture."

Syd nodded. "Sure. Or else he's hosing you. Softening you up so you let him stay longer. Smart idea—start a project you can't possibly finish in two weeks."

"That's pretty cynical," I said, stung.

Syd shrugged. "It's realistic."

"Hey, Andy!" Silas called. "Almost time to get those tomato plants!"

"Be right with you," I shouted back.

Syd leaned in closer. "Remember when you were going to try to find out what really happened?" she asked in a low voice. "Why did you back-burner the idea? Are you afraid of what you'll find?"

"No," I said. "Of course not!"

"Then why don't you do it?" Syd asked.

"I'm going to do it," I said.

"Andy!" Silas called.

"You're being paged," Syd said in a disgusted voice. "I guess I took too much of your time."

"I'll call you," I said. Syd waved over her shoulder, but didn't look back.

I stood until she disappeared around the corner of the house. Silas came and stood next to me.

"Can't let them get to you, kiddo," he said softly.

"Them?" I asked, still looking at the empty air.

"Women." In a sudden movement, he buried the tip of the shovel into the lawn, then wiped his hands on his pants. "Can't let them push you around."

"What do you mean?" I asked, turning to face him. "Syd doesn't push me around."

He smiled. "They all do it. They just do it smart, so you don't notice. Just stand your ground," he said. "That's all I'm saying."

Then his green eyes twinkled. "Then again, some things are worth getting pushed around for."

"Syd and I are just friends," I said frostily.

"So what was the problem?" he asked. His green eyes fixed on me with concern. "She seemed upset."

"I guess I'd made plans with her and forgot about it," I said.

"That's never wise," Silas said. "She didn't seem too happy with me, either."

"Well, you know," I said, shrugging. "I guess Syd and her mom are worried about you showing up. They don't know you, and they know . . . they know you've been in prison. You can see how that would be."

He nodded, staring past me back at the

garden. "Hey. Anybody ever call you Mac?"

I shook my head. "Just Andy."

"I'm going to call you Mac," he said. "Rocket was a name for a kid. I might slip and call you that sometimes. But I like Mac. Suits you. Okay, Mac?"

"A nickname," I said. "I've never had one, except for Beanhead."

"Beanhead?"

"Syd calls me that. Once, I ate this truly gross amount of three-bean salad back when we were younger."

"Ah. Syd sure likes to cut you down to size, doesn't she?"

"What do you mean?" I asked.

"Nothing." He clapped me on the shoulder. "So, you ready to hit the greenhouse, Mac?"

"Sure." We walked off together, our steps in sync. His hand felt warm on my shoulder. And I had a nickname. A good, strong name, strong as a handshake. Mac.

11//murder most foul

To: rcktman
From: grossgrrl
Subject: infantile behavior

fighting like that reminds me of that time we were around eleven. we tied in a race, and i couldn't stand it, and i said i won. and you said i couldn't stand losing. and i said you couldn't stand being wrong.

you still can't stand being wrong. and i still can't stand losing. but i hate wasting time. wanna come over and make up?

I waited a day.
She opened her door and gave me that Syd eyebrow-lift that meant *it's about time.*

"Hey," I said.

"Hey," she said.

Ah, teenage conversation. You just can't beat it for sparkle, can you?

"Okay, you were right," I said. "I do hate being wrong. And I did stop the Silas investigation as soon as he came to town. I dropped the ball."

"That's not unusual," Syd said with a smirk. "I still remember last summer's Verona championship softball game."

Every summer, the local companies in Verona hold a charity softball game. Mom and Rachel's company always play, and last year, Rachel, Syd, and I were on the team. I guess I had bobbled a few balls, but Syd hadn't been that great, either.

"Hardy har," I said. "Look who's talking. Where have you gone, Joe DiMaggio?"

"Hey, I'm the one who stole second," Syd said. "You're the one who dropped the high fly."

"Are you going to let me in, or are you going to broadcast my lack of athletic ability to the entire neighborhood?" I asked.

Syd stood aside. At least I was allowed in her house again.

I walked into the living room. Everything in it is beige. About a year ago, Rachel hired this woman from the city to come up and redo the house in all natural materials. She'd stripped paint and torn out any plastic or fiberglass insulation. Syd and I called her the Toxic Avenger.

I flopped down on the all-natural couch. "Got any chemicals in a can, like a soda?" I asked.

"Nope, just herbal tea, and don't get comfortable," Syd said. "I have stuff for you. Come on."

I followed her into her bedroom. Syd's room is the only colorful one in the house, filled with deep colors, like gold and rose and purple—all natural dyes, of course. Her desk was piled high with papers.

"Have you been doing homework during school break?" I asked. "That isn't like you, Syd. Are you feeling okay?"

Syd swept the papers into a pile and dumped them in my lap. "They're your *dad's* trial transcripts. I got them from

Dolores. I thought you might want to read them."

I looked at the papers. I swallowed.

"Unless you're afraid to," Syd said.

I started to read.

I read every page. It took me the rest of the afternoon. Syd reread some pages and kept me supplied with iced tea and "healthy" oatmeal raisin cookies.

It wasn't pleasure reading. In the medical examiner's testimony, I had to read details of my birth mother's injuries, details I'd rather not know about. Sometimes I had to stop, close my eyes, and take a breath.

"Don't read that part," Syd said. She held out her hand for the paper.

"It's okay," I said. "I want to know."

Finally, I was done. It was late afternoon. Syd sat on the bed cross-legged and fixed me with her dark, steady gaze.

"So," she said.

"So," I said. I lifted one shoulder in a shrug. "Now I know everything."

"And?"

"And I still don't know anything," I said.

Syd bounced up on the bed. "How can you say that? It's all here!"

"What's all here?" I countered. "Two lawyers twisting the facts to fit their own scenario. It doesn't tell me anything!"

Syd walked on her knees across the bed. She riffled through the pages on the desk.

"Their next-door neighbor testified that she heard them arguing. And Pam said that Silas wouldn't let Pam get a driver's license," Syd said. "He was controlling!"

"He was protective," I said, pointing to Silas's testimony. "It was winter, and Pam herself was afraid of driving in snow. He said he'd give her lessons in the spring."

Frustrated, Syd ran her hands through her hair. Her bangs stuck straight up. "Pam's dentist testified that she begged him not to send a bill for that broken tooth to the house. She'd walk to the office and pay it off slowly. He said she appeared *terrified* of her husband."

"First of all, she was really shy," I said. "That kind of behavior can be totally misinterpreted. Second of all, they were having a hard time with money. She was trying to *protect* Silas so that he wouldn't worry about the bill."

"She's not allowed to go to the dentist?" Syd yelled.

I took a deep breath so that I wouldn't yell back. "Silas didn't know about it, Syd. You read his testimony. If he had, he would have been happy to pay the bill and drive her there."

"What about the broken tooth?" Syd demanded. "She also had bruises on her face."

"She fell on the ice! She told people that!"

Syd shook her head. "Don't you see it, Andy?" she asked. Her voice was soft now. "They had a weird, confining marriage. They never went out together. I know they didn't have much money. But the neighbors never once saw them in the backyard, or taking a walk, or loading the car for a picnic, or a trip. Not in the two years they lived there. Don't you think that's weird?"

"How should I know?" I asked. My voice rose. I was tired of Syd's insinuations. "They were acting newlyweddy. They wanted to be alone. They had a bunch of nosy neighbors! But everybody liked Silas—he was friendly and polite when they ran into him in town. Nobody was afraid of him."

"Except Pam," Syd said grimly. "Okay, what about Ham Jernigan?" She sprang forward and began searching through the papers again. "Silas thought she was having an affair with him—he admitted that on the stand, after his coworker testified that Silas followed them one day. Jernigan said Pam saw Silas spying on them, and she was"—Syd searched the transcript—"'*Visibly* terrified.' Terrified, Andy!"

"Because she was afraid he'd find out she was cheating!" I burst out. "What wife wouldn't be scared?"

"But she *wasn't* cheating!" Syd said. "You can tell by the transcript. This Ham Jernigan guy really sounds to me like he was telling the truth."

"What are you, psychic?" I asked scornfully. "You can tell when someone is telling the truth?"

"Everyone on this planet can tell better

than you!" Syd shot back. "A *monkey* would have more perception!"

"Thanks a lot," I said. "And you are totally unbiased, right?"

Syd stuck her chin at me. "Would you listen to Ham Jernigan? He's still alive."

I shrugged.

"We could search for him on the Net," Syd said.

"Why should we bother?" I said. "He'll just say the same things he did on the stand."

"But there might be things he wasn't *allowed* to say," Syd pointed out. "Stuff that's hearsay, or inadmissible. I think we should find out where he is now."

"Syd, this is crazy," I said, my voice rising. "I forbid you to look for Jernigan."

"You *forbid* me?" Syd's eyebrows rose. "Did I just hear that?"

"Look, this is my problem, okay?" I said. "And we're getting nowhere. There's just no way of knowing what really happened."

"You don't want to know what really happened!" Syd cried.

I gathered up all the papers in a ball and stuffed them into my backpack. I didn't want Syd poring over them like a maniac, looking for more reasons to incriminate my dad.

"The doubt isn't going to go away, Syd," I said. "Sometimes you just have to have faith in a person."

"He's really got you," she whispered. "He really does. And Wendy is falling for it, too. Mom thinks—"

"You've been discussing us?" I asked.

"Well, she read the transcript, too," Syd admitted. "And she thinks your mom is vulnerable to this kind of man. I hate to say it, Andy, but Wendy can be a real sap."

"I forgot," I said. I slapped my head. "This is the house of know-it-alls."

"That's not fair, Andy," Syd said angrily. "Just because we don't agree with—"

But, suddenly, the door slammed, and we heard angry voices. Syd and I stopped arguing to listen.

"If that's the way you feel, why didn't you say something before?" It was my mom. Her voice was high-pitched and choked with emotion. "Instead, you go behind my back—"

"For the last time, Wendy, I didn't go behind your back," Rachel answered angrily. "I was going to talk to you about it today, okay? You really have to get a handle on your betrayal issues."

"Don't psychoanalyze me!" Mom yelled. "I'm tired of it!"

"You weren't so tired of it over the last ten years, when you'd run to me every time you had a problem with a man," Rachel countered. "And, believe me, you kept me busy!"

Syd and I moved quickly down the hall and hurried into the living room.

"What's going on?" Syd asked, looking from her mom's cool, determined fury to my mom's flushed face.

"We're having an argument about work, honey," Rachel answered. "Nothing to worry about—"

"There is something to worry about," Mom said grimly. "Because I don't know if I can trust you anymore, Rachel."

"Oh, and you can trust that *murderer*

you let into your home?" Rachel asked sarcastically.

"Wait a second," I said.

Mom held up her hand. "It's okay, Andy. I can handle this."

"You can handle this?" Rachel asked incredulously. "Wake up and smell the decaf, Wendy. You're being conned!"

"So is Andy," Syd piped up. "He refuses to face facts."

I went to stand beside Mom. She turned to Rachel and Syd. "Whether we trust Silas Murdoch or not is none of your business," she said, her voice shaking. "And you can stop looking down on us for having a little trust in people. That's better than being cynical—"

"Try smart!" Rachel yelled.

"I don't have to listen to this," Mom said. She whirled around and stalked to the door. I hurried after her. The door banged shut behind us. The sound seemed to echo. It sounded hollow and final, too. Like it was the end of something.

12//blood

When we got outside, Mom and I stopped in the driveway next to her car. For a long moment, we just looked at each other. We were thinking the same thing. We'd never fought with Rachel and Syd before. Not like that.

Sure, we'd argued about which movie to see on Saturday night. Or whether to go to the Mexican restaurant, or order in Chinese. Syd and I had no shortage of opinions, and neither did Mom and Rachel.

But this was different.

Mom's hand was shaking as she put the key in the lock of the car door. "I've got to go back to work, Andy," she said.

"Mom, you're super upset," I said.

"Maybe you should call it a day."

She shook her head. "I've got to call a lawyer. Rachel already hired her own attorney. Can you imagine that? She doesn't trust me. He said she deserves more royalties on one of our CD-ROM games. I mean, she always handled most of the creative part, and I did the business. But I thought we were fifty-fifty partners."

"You were," I said. "I can't believe Rachel is going to do that."

"Well, she didn't say she was," Mom said. "But that's what she means." She rubbed her forehead. "Silas warned me this might happen."

"Silas? How did he get involved?"

"He's not involved," Mom said. "He just . . . gave a word to the wise, that's all. And he was right. I do need my own lawyer. Conflict of interest is written all over this thing."

I wasn't quite getting it. I was no business whiz. But the bottom line was that Mom didn't trust Rachel anymore.

Mom patted my shoulder. "Do you want to come with me, sweetie? You can hang in the conference room and watch TV. Silas is painting the back room at the house. The whole place smells like paint."

"That's okay, I don't mind," I said. "I'm going to head home."

Mom got in the car and drove off. I frowned, thinking. It was kind of weird that Silas would talk to Mom about her business—and that she would listen.

I got on my bike and pedaled home, down the route I had ridden probably thousands of times.

For years, Mom and I had called Syd and Rachel our "family." It was the four of us against the world.

But they weren't our family. They weren't blood.

Silas was.

Mom had wanted to paint the back room for ages, and even offered to pay me to do it, but we both kept putting it off. It had once been an outdoor porch that a former owner had enclosed. There was a wall of windows looking out to the backyard, and it was the sunniest room in the house. Mom had wanted to paint it yellow, the golden yellow of a buttercup, she said.

When I got home, Silas had finished painting the walls and had started painting the floorboards white. The windows were open, and a breeze swept all the way through the house, thanks to the propped-open front door.

I carefully kept to the unpainted part of the floor and watched Silas for a moment.

"Hey, Mac," Silas said as he rolled the paint over the boards. "How does it look?"

"Great," I said.

"Think I got more paint on me than the walls," he said, grinning and pointing to his work boots, which were speckled with yellow and white paint.

I felt better, just standing there, watching him paint. I wished Rachel and Syd could see how generous he was. Mom hadn't asked him to paint the room. He saw that it needed it, and he asked her what color she'd like. That was the way he did things. He didn't call attention to anything he did, or make you feel like you had to thank him a thousand times. "It's nothing," he'd say.

"Took me a morning. And I need to stretch my muscles." That's the way he handled it.

"I bet you could use a soda, or some iced tea," I said.

"Now, how'd you know that? I sure have worked up a thirst," Silas said. "I think Wendy made some iced tea this morning with that fresh mint I brought over yesterday."

"One tall one, coming up," I said.

Since Silas had moved out most of the furniture, I perched my backpack on the step of the ladder. I headed out to the kitchen and poured the tea over ice cubes in a tall glass. Then I headed back to the porch.

Silas was standing in the middle of the room, holding the papers from my backpack. I took in the scene in a glance. I saw where he'd walked in the wet paint and left a footprint. I saw my backpack overturned on the floor. One of the pages had stuck to the freshly painted floor.

I saw what had happened. The backpack must have tipped over. The zipper's busted, so papers must have spilled, and maybe a gust of wind had sent them flying. Silas had dropped his brush and hurried to retrieve them. Some of them had stuck to the wet paint.

Now, he was reading them.

I froze, my fingers slick against the wet glass. Silas looked up at me. His eyes were dead. I'd never seen him look like that before. "You're checking up on me, boy?" he asked.

13//in the name of the father

"N-no," I said quickly. "I'm not check—"

"Then what are my trial transcripts doing in your backpack, Andy?" Silas asked. His voice was calm and cool, and his expression never changed.

"I got them from"—I was about to say "Syd," but I still wanted Silas and Syd to get along—"Someone," I blurted. "It doesn't matter who. But the reason I wanted them was to see if I could find a clue. Something that was overlooked. A clue that could clear you."

"So who's the someone who can get trial transcripts?" Silas asked.

"There's this victims' rights advocate in town," I said. "She knows all that stuff." I didn't want to mention Syd, and besides, Dolores was the one who had gotten the transcripts.

"It's public information," I added lamely.

Suddenly, Silas threw the papers at me, right in my face. The jerky movement startled me, and I reared back, spilling the iced tea.

"That's what it means," Silas said. "Feathers in a windstorm."

He turned and walked to the corner. He picked up his roller again. He dipped it in the paint, but he didn't start to work again.

"Public information," he said, staring at the roller. "That's right. Your name gets dragged through the mud, and anybody can read it, anytime. They can listen to what other folks thought about your marriage, and what kind of husband you were. Public information."

"I'm sorry, Silas," I said.

He sighed. "I'm not mad at you, Rocket. I get upset when the past comes back. Seeing it in black and white, the words, the accusations, after all this time. . . . I don't want to think about it. It's all I thought about for fourteen long years. You know what? Here's something crazy. Part of me thought I'd get out of prison and Pam would be waiting for me. Just as pretty as a picture, like she always was."

Silas looked up at me. His eyes were filled with tears. I was shocked to see them. Silas was not the type of man who cried.

"I loved her so much," he said.

The moment spun out between us like a single golden thread. The sun flooded the room, and the paint was like gold. There were no shadows anywhere. There was nowhere to hide. And finally, finally, I could ask the question I'd been dying to ask since he'd come.

"What was she like?"

Silas's expression was faraway. "She was sweet. Quiet. She was a waitress when I met her, but she was never one for chitchat. She'd smile and say good morning, and pour your coffee, and that was it. I fell for her by the time I stood up to pay my bill."

He put the roller back in the pan and wiped his hands on his jeans.

"I know we got married too young. Pam,

especially—she was only nineteen. But we were in love. And she wanted to. She didn't have much ambition, your mom. She just wanted a home. She had a tough childhood, and her parents died when she was a teenager, both of them, one after the other. Maybe that's why Pam worried so much, about everything. About the mortgage, about bills, about my having enough work. She was the champ of worrying, all right. That was her only fault. Well, that and her tendency to give people the benefit of the doubt. She was way too kind. That's why she let those boys in the house. You could talk her into anything."

Silas's face grew hard. "She should have said no. For once in her life, she should have said no."

I wondered what it would have been like, to grow up with a different mom. A mom who wasn't a businessperson. A mom who just wanted to make a home.

As if he were reading my thoughts, Silas said, "Pam was a one hundred eighty from your mom. You couldn't get more different. Wendy's a tough lady. But that's good,

Rocket. She's had to raise you alone. She's needed to be."

He looked at me across the room. "I'm grateful to her. She raised you right. You're a lucky kid."

And you know what? For the first time in what seemed like forever, I felt that I was, too.

Even though I knew that I was totally right and Syd was totally wrong, my conscience bothered me. I had fought with Syd plenty of times, but never like this. Besides, I missed her.

I took the car and stopped by her house, but no one was home. I decided to cruise around town to look for her. I tried the bookstore, video store, and even parked and poked my head in a couple of Syd's favorite cafés. *Nada*.

She could be out for a long bike ride. I headed the car down Further Road, which ran along the meadows outside of town. Just at the town's outskirts was a greasy spoon called the Willow Bay Diner.

I checked the windows as I drove by, just

in case Syd had stopped for a cold drink. I did a double take and nearly drove off the road.

Because I didn't see Syd. I saw Rachel. And Silas. They were sitting in a booth.

I drove past, then made a U-turn and went back, just to make sure. And it was them, huddled together in conversation.

Seriously strange.

I could stew about it, and cook up all kinds of theories, but I did the easy thing and asked Silas. As soon as I saw him return to the garage apartment, I went over and knocked on his door.

I told him what I'd seen. Of course, it was none of my business . . . but why?

Silas didn't seem surprised at the question. He sighed. "It is your business, Rocket," he said. "Well, it's your mom's. Maybe I shouldn't have butted in. But I hate to see Wendy so unhappy, you know?"

I knew. When Mom is unhappy, nothing is right. She is not one of those people who believes in putting on a good front.

"Rachel asked me out for coffee. She

thought maybe a neutral person could refer-ee the situation."

"So what happened?" I asked.

Silas shook his head sadly. "I'm afraid that woman won't budge. She *says* she wants to be fair to Wendy, but"—he shrugged—"Let's just say they have irrecon-cilable differences. Rachel feels she's con-tributed more to the company, and that's it. It looks like they're going to have to sell the business. They can't work together."

Silas put a hand on my shoulder. "Listen, Rocket, do me a favor, okay? Don't tell Wendy about this. She'd think I was inter-fering, and she'd be right. I defended your mom, and I sure didn't make things better. She'd just get upset all over again. We have to protect her, you and me. So promise?"

"I promise," I said. I felt weird keeping something from my mom. But Silas was right. It would just upset her again.

I left and went back to the house. But I couldn't help thinking about how strange the encounter was in the first place. Rachel hadn't pulled any punches the other day. It was clear that she thought Silas was a sleazy, homicidal user. The chances of her listening to him were about less than zero.

So why would she ask him for advice? Maybe it was just a ploy. Had she and Syd hatched a plan to come between Silas and Wendy?

14//the evil within

To: grossgrrl
From: rcktman
Subject: wanna?

I don't know who's right, and I don't care. I just wanna be friends. Wanna?

To: rcktman
From: grossgrrl
Subject: give it a try

will you kneel and ask my forgiveness? i didn't think so. how about . . . we don't talk about silas?

you know what emotional trauma does to me, macfarland. meet ya there, 12pm.

@ @ @

Syd was waiting for me at the Red Bird Café.

"Maybe we shouldn't talk about the Moms' fight, either," Syd said. "I'm sensing minefields everywhere."

"So let's just eat," I suggested.

Eating is something that Syd and I are very, very good at. We managed to get through an entire cheeseburger lunch without bringing up Silas.

We talked about movies we wanted to see, and what a drag it was that school would be starting the next day. It was an okay time, but it was like there was a giant pink elephant in the room that we didn't talk about. I wasn't used to awkward silences with Syd. It made me feel funny and lost.

After lunch, we stood by our bikes out on the sidewalk. After that lead-balloon lunch, you'd think we'd be anxious to go our separate ways. But we both lingered, practically stubbing our toes in the dirt like little kids.

Finally, I remembered that I was the guy.

I should take some initiative. "Want to go for a bike ride?" I suggested.

Syd shrugged. "Sure."

Her reply wasn't exactly brimming with enthusiasm, but I'd take what I could get.

Syd led the way as we rode down Main Street, then turned off on a little-traveled road that's lined with warehouses. It's a shortcut to a state park that has nifty bike trails.

Suddenly, Syd hit the brakes. I almost pitched onto her back tire.

"What are you doing?" I asked.

"Shhh," Syd said. She quickly bumped her bike over the curb and led it into the shadow of a warehouse. She beckoned to me. "Hurry!" she whispered.

I followed her, drawing into the cool shade. She put her lips close to my ear. "Halfway down the block. To the left. I don't think they saw us."

Two men were standing, talking, by the side of a warehouse. Even though he had his back to me, I recognized Silas. I couldn't really see the other man. His face was in shadow.

"So?" I said. "Silas is talking to someone. Isn't he allowed?" But my voice was nervous, and Syd lifted an eyebrow at me.

"So, maybe nothing," she said. "But it looks pretty intense."

Syd was right. Even though I couldn't see Silas's face, I could tell by the way he was standing that he wasn't relaxed. The other guy waved his arms, as if to try to placate Silas.

"What's going on, do you think?" Syd whispered, peering at Silas.

"Maybe he's asking for a job in one of these warehouses," I suggested. "He's been applying at restaurants all over town."

"So he said."

"Don't start with me." I kept my eyes on the two men. It sure didn't look like a job interview. But I wasn't going to correct what I'd said. Syd wasn't lying when she said I hate to admit when I'm wrong.

"Maybe we can get closer to hear them," Syd said. "There's an alley that runs behind those buildings."

I didn't get a chance to say yes or no. Silas and the other guy split up. Silas headed down the street, and the other guy started toward us.

Syd tugged at my arm, and we quickly moved to the side of the building. We watched the other man walk down the opposite sidewalk. He was tall and slim, dressed in gray pants and a plaid shirt. He was bald, with a fringe of hair around his ears. In other words, he was a perfectly ordinary guy. He strolled down the street, turned the corner, and disappeared.

"Let's follow him," Syd hissed.

"Wait a—" I started.

But Syd had already taken off.

There's an advantage to being a kid on a bike. You might as well be wearing an invisible cloak. You're part of the scenery, and nobody notices you. You're just a kid on a bike.

So our guy wasn't suspicious at all. He didn't even notice us. We stayed well behind him, but kept him in sight. It helped that we know Verona like the back of our hands.

We followed him to the Butternut Motel, the same place Silas had stayed. He turned the key to room fourteen and went inside.

"Now what?" Syd said.

"I wish we knew who he was," I said. "Or at least his name."

"If we knew his name, Dolores could find out other stuff about him," Syd said.

"Maybe I should just ask Silas," I suggested.

"Good idea, Andy," Syd said sarcastically. *"Um, Silas? Who's that person that you set up a secret meeting with?* Then see if he tells you the truth."

"We don't know it was a secret meeting!"

"Yeah, right," Syd said. "Everybody meets on that block. It's such a charming spot."

The girl could definitely irritate me with two hands tied behind her back. "Do you have any better ideas?" I asked.

Syd flashed me a cocky grin. "Always. Do you have your shades with you?"

"Why?" I asked suspiciously.

Syd strode into the tiny office of the motel. A gray-haired guy with a very red nose was reading a hot-rod magazine. He wasn't the desk clerk I'd asked about Silas, so I breathed a sigh of relief.

We stood there, but he didn't look up.

"Be with you in a minute."

"I certainly hope so," Syd answered in a clipped tone. "Because I do believe your place has the right kind of *uncouth* charm for what we need."

That made him look up. Syd cruised the office, not meeting his eye. A few moments ago, outside, she had dumped water on her hands from a bottle in her backpack and slicked back her black hair. She'd put on my pair of cool black shades and rolled up the sleeves of her black T-shirt. She had put on red lipstick. It's truly amazing what's in a girl's backpack.

Then she squinted at me, told me I was hopeless, and dug in her backpack again. She put her baseball cap on my head backwards and told me to keep my mouth shut and slouch.

"Desiree Domino, advance man," Syd said to the clerk.

"Advance man for what?" he asked.

"Clampett, Hathaway, and Drysdale," Syd said. At the blank look on the man's face, she added, "Advertising agency? You've heard of us, of course."

"Of course," he said.

"We're scouting locations for a shoot," Syd said. "This place just could be ideal. Is the owner available, by the way?"

The man hitched up his pants. "I'm the owner. Mike Pishkin."

"Fabulous. Mr. Pishkin, we'd need to book the entire motel for . . . oh, three days, minimum. On March tenth, eleventh, and twelfth. Can do?"

I gazed at Syd in admiration. It was amazing. I'd never met an advertising person in my life, but I'm sure they look and sound just like Syd did.

"Let me check the book." Mike Pishkin hurried to the desk. The Butternut Motel had most likely never flashed that NO VACANCY sign. He'd more likely have to check the bulbs.

From my vantage point, I watched Pishkin flip over empty page after empty page. "Hmmm. I think we do have an opening.

Seeing that you came so far in advance. We book up, though."

"I'll bet you do," Syd said brightly. "May I see a room?"

"Sure." He pushed over a key. "Number eleven is empty."

So were numbers one through ten, and twelve through thirteen. But, wisely, Syd did not point this out.

She hesitated, the key in her hand. "Aren't you coming with me?" she asked Pishkin.

"Don't need to. There's a bed and a chair, and a, you know, bathroom," he said. "They're all the same. I don't like to leave the front desk. Because of the traffic."

Syd flicked her gaze to the empty road outside the window. "But I have thousands of *questions*," she said.

She sighed, and looked at me. "I don't know, Dmitri. Maybe we should go upscale. Just think how Cindy would react to this place. We'll have another screaming episode on our hands, it will take up half a day, and we're paying her a *fortune*." She rolled her eyes. "Supermodels! If it isn't the six-packs of Evian, it's the lettuce flown in from France, and they still pitch a fit!"

Pishkin licked his lips. "Cindy?"

"Crawford," Syd said. "Come on, Dmitri."

"Wait!" Mike Pishkin said. "I guess it would be okay to leave the office empty for a minute." He hurried around the desk, smashing his knee into a chair on the way. He didn't seem to feel it. He limped toward Syd, a big smile on his face.

"Dmitri, you'd better stay here and make those calls. You can use my cell." Syd gave me a meaningful look, cutting her eyes toward the register. I nodded.

As soon as they left, I sped over to the desk and spun the register toward me. There was only one name on it.

Bob Treat

Bob Treat! The manager of The Happy Sole, back in Bangor, Maine! What was he doing here in California?

I spun the book around, then hurriedly took a seat on the only chair. I picked up a hot-rod magazine and flipped through it. In only a few minutes, Syd was back.

"Didn't I mention we ab-so-lutely must have one?" Syd was saying as she came through the door. "I thought I did . . . oh, well."

"B-but I can't put in a Jacuzzi, just for you!"

"Pity," Syd said. "What can you do? Search on, search on."

She signaled to me, and we beat it out the door just as Pishkin called, "Give my regards to Cindy!"

"Bob Treat? Wow," Syd said slowly. "What the heck would Silas be doing talking to the guy who fired him?"

We had ridden as fast as we could back toward town, and now we were walking our bikes.

"You know, we said we wouldn't talk about Silas today," I started.

"But, Andy, we bumped right into this!"

"Hang on, will you? I'm not finished." I took a breath. "But since he's the topic at the moment, I really need to ask you something."

"So ask."

"Is Rachel going behind Mom's back and pulling some kind of trick on Silas?" I asked. "I saw her talking to him. Is there some kind of plan in the works?"

Syd stopped walking. "Some kind of plan?" she asked icily. "What are you saying? That my mom is working behind the scenes to sabotage your mom? That we're both lying to you?"

"Oh, like she isn't doing that already with the business?" I said. "She hired her own lawyer!"

"Your mom did, too! And she did it first!" Syd yelled. "What is with you, Andy? I try to be nice, try to understand that you've got this major father issue going—"

"I don't have a father *issue,* I have a *father!*" I said. "And I don't need your niceness, or your help. I just need you to butt out!"

Syd's mouth flattened into a thin line. "Fine. I'll butt out."

She swung her leg over her bike and took off. "Forever!" she yelled.

I had found Silas digging holes for the

tomato plants. He'd already planted a row, and I remembered guiltily that I had promised to help him instead of running around trying to collect evidence against him.

And all that time, he was working in the hot sun, making my mom's dream of a garden come true.

Take that, Syd!

"What's up, Mac?" Silas asked. "You look like you just fell into a nest of fire ants."

"I had a fight with Syd," I mumbled. "For, like, the thirty-seventh time in two weeks."

"Ah. Want to talk about it?"

"Not really," I said. I kicked at a clod of dirt.

"'Kay." Silas dug up a spadeful of earth. "If you want some advice about women, though, I'll give you some for free. A woman's got a way of finding your soft spot. Then they stick a stiletto in it. So never apologize. Never explain."

Syd's sardonic voice floated in my head. *Great advice. For a sociopath.*

But I hadn't come to talk about Syd. I'd come to talk about Bob Treat.

"Do you have a friend in town?" I asked.

He stopped working. "A friend?"

"From Maine?"

He dug a hole and planted another plant. "Who told you that, the crazy lady with the newsletter?"

"No, I saw you," I said. "On Case Street. You were talking to some guy. I called, but you didn't hear me."

Silas looked up. His face was red, but I think it was from the sun and digging. "Yeah, I ran into an old pal. Could have knocked me over with a feather."

"Who was he?" I held my breath.

"Bob Treat," Silas said easily. He leaned on the shovel.

"Bob Treat!" I said, trying to act surprised. "Why would he look you up? Wasn't he your boss? He fired you!"

"Bob didn't fire me—he was just the manager. The owner fired me," Silas explained. "Bob tried to cover for me about my record. When the owner found out, he fired *him*. So I owe the guy one for trying."

"Are you two good pals?" I asked.

Silas shrugged. "Not really. I was surprised to see him, to tell you the truth. But he'd always wanted to come to California, get a fresh start. He was jealous when I took off. And he figured there'd be plenty of restaurant jobs around here. That's what we were talking about. I was telling him that I was beating my head against plenty of doors, let me tell you. This here is no promised land."

"So what's he going to do?"

Silas shrugged again. "Don't know. Said he was going to try for work in Napa. I'm not too worried about him, Mac. He's got a nest egg. He's ten steps ahead of me, let me tell you. But you know what he doesn't have? Family. Which means I'm a hundred steps ahead of him."

He smiled at me then. You have to understand about Silas's smile. It took in the world, and it took you in, too. You felt included. Special. And all your doubts just flew away.

Later that evening, Dolores knocked on

my door. Silas was still out back, and I was setting the table for dinner. Surprised, I asked her inside.

She perched on the edge of a chair, looking nervous.

"What is it, Dolores?" I asked gently.

"I came to tell you that I'm going to have to mail you that information," she said. "I'll do it, don't worry. But I'm going to have to mail it."

"What information, Dolores?" I was confused.

"On that Treat person. Bob Treat." Dolores wiped her hands on her jeans.

"I didn't ask for . . . "

"Your friend. Syd. She asked."

Syd. I felt angry all over again.

"So I came to tell you that, and get your address. And to tell you . . . tell you"—she wrung her hands in her lap—"That I'm leaving town," she blurted.

I sat down opposite her and leaned forward. I realized that she looked scared.

"What is it, Dolores?" I asked. "Are you afraid of something?"

She fixed her milky eyes on me.

"Someone is going to kill me, Andrew," she whispered.

Whoa. Talk about paranoia!

"What makes you think that?" I asked carefully.

She shook her head back and forth. "Town is dangerous. I'm going to live in the mountains."

"Which mountains?" I asked.

"Away from everyone," Dolores continued. "I don't like abandoning Verona. I'm letting everyone down. They depend on me—"

"So maybe you should stay," I said, even though if the town knew that Dolores was leaving, they'd probably hire a brass band to send her on her way.

She leaned closer and grabbed my knee. Her nails scratched against the denim. "Nobody is safe here, Andrew. Don't let down your guard. The evil is without and within!"

Just then, the faint chink of metal was carried on the breeze. It was Silas, still planting in the garden.

Dolores jumped to her feet. She ran to the back window and peered outside.

"Dolores, relax," I said, following her.

"I'd better go. I—"

Suddenly, she drew back, hiding behind the curtain. "Who is that?" she asked fearfully.

"It's just our houseguest, Dolores." I crossed to the window and looked out. "He's gardening. Nothing to worry about."

I had never told Dolores that the man she had researched was now staying with us. I didn't want to send her over the edge.

Silas was in shadow. He straightened, facing the house, and Dolores quickly ducked back.

Her eyes were wild. "It's the devil!" she told me.

"Dolores, relax," I said. "I told you—"

She ran back through the living room, toward the front door. She opened it and whirled around to face me.

"It's the devil next door!" she cried.

She ran out, banging the door behind her.

I shook my head. Poor Dolores had finally lost her grip.

15//i told you i was sick

Syd didn't e-mail me that night. I didn't e-mail her, either. The next day at school we totally avoided each other. I didn't think that we'd make up very easily this time. Cheeseburgers can't take care of everything. It didn't help that our moms weren't speaking, either.

The church was running its annual rummage sale, and Mom always used it as an opportunity to "hone down," as she called it. We went through all our clothes and old coats, even our shoes, and gave away anything we hadn't worn in the past year. It was a major chore, and Mom usually had to feed me a whole batch of chocolate chip cookies just to get my enthusiasm up to lukewarm.

That night we were sorting sweaters into "toss it" and "keep it for another year" piles when someone pounded on our door. I went to open it, and it was Syd. Had she come to apologize, or beat me up?

But Syd wasn't thinking about our fight. She grabbed my hand. "Andy," she said breathlessly. "Dolores is dead!"

It had happened the night before. Dolores had called 911 around one in the morning, saying that someone was trying to break in. She was hysterical. Unfortunately, she had tried to shoot the burglar and had shot herself instead.

The police still weren't sure if there was an actual burglar or an imagined one. There was no evidence of a lock being forced. The door was found wide open, but Dolores could have done that. There were footprints by the window, but they could have been left by the man who had cut Dolores's grass and clipped her hedges. They were checking on it.

"It's funny, isn't it?" Syd said in a far-away voice. "She was afraid of criminals all her life, and one got her in the end. It's like that guy whose epitaph was, 'I Told You I Was Sick.'"

I went to the funeral on Wednesday with Syd. We didn't even mention our fight. It seemed pretty stupid now.

Practically the whole town showed up for the funeral. I saw Mom slip in with Silas in the back. She nodded at Rachel, who'd come with a neighbor. Syd and I sat together, holding hands.

After the service, Syd and I stopped to talk to Dolores's only relative, her sister, Belinda. She had driven all the way from Nevada to see to her sister's arrangements. She looked a little like Dolores, the kind of woman who felt more comfortable in jeans than in a dress.

When I told her my name, she held on to my hand.

"Andrew MacFarland," she murmured. "I know your name. I think I saw it on the papers on Dolores's desk. . . . "

"I'd asked for her help on something," I said. "She was a very nice person."

Okay, it sounded lame. But everything sounds lame at a funeral.

Belinda gave me a small, wry smile, as if she knew that Dolores only dipped one oar in the water half the time. "She *was* a very nice person. You should have known her when she was younger. Thanks for saying that."

We all walked to the cemetery, which was in the churchyard. There was a short service, and then Dolores's casket was lowered into the earth.

It was a beautiful day. Birds were singing, and the sun was shining on the green leaves and the grass. Syd gripped my hand hard. It was funny how bad we both felt for Dolores. I'm not sure how much we had even liked her when she was alive. Now, all of a sudden, I was regretting that I'd never really talked to her. I'd just asked her for things. And how crazy was she? Not so very, it turned out.

Funerals are not only about lame remarks. They're about kicking yourself for the things you should have done.

Afterward, some of the adults went up to

Belinda and asked her back to their place for coffee. Belinda thanked everyone politely, but said she'd rather just go back to Dolores's place and pack. She was in a hurry to get back to her ranch.

I waited for Mom, who went up to Belinda with Silas. I saw Mom introduce Silas, then launch into one of those "if there's anything I can do" speeches.

But Belinda wasn't paying attention to Mom. She was staring at Silas.

"I know you," she said. She didn't say it loudly, but her voice was strong, and in the quiet graveyard, it carried. "I read all about you. Dolores had collected stories."

"Belinda, Silas is my houseguest," Mom said gently. "I really think—"

"You're letting him stay in your *house?*" Belinda's voice rose, and people stopped moving toward their cars to listen. "Look, I don't know you, but maybe you should take a look at what Dolores has—"

"I've seen it," Mom answered coolly.

Belinda turned her gaze onto Silas. "You better not have had anything to do with my sister's death, mister."

"Hold on here," Silas said. "I never even met your sister. I'm just here to support Wendy and Andy."

Belinda looked over at me. Then she looked back at Silas. "I know my sister was afraid of you," she said. "And I know you're a convicted murderer."

A gasp rose from the group in the cemetery. I closed my eyes. Great. Now everyone in town would know.

"So if you put two and two together, what do you get?" Belinda asked.

"Zero," Silas said softly. "Sometimes, you get zero. Come on, Wendy."

There wasn't one bit of evidence against him. But within days, every person in town suspected Silas Murdoch of murdering Dolores Sakonnet.

Even the police came calling. Silas answered their questions patiently. I watched them, in the backyard. At least they didn't take him downtown.

Then the police talked to us. We couldn't exactly vouch for Silas, since Dolores had been killed at one in the morning and we were all in bed. But we swore that Silas had gone back to his apartment, and Wendy had said that she'd seen the light go out right around when she went to bed, at midnight.

Which meant exactly squat.

"So what do you think?" Syd asked me.

I was stuffing clothes into Hefty bags after school on Friday. Even Silas had contributed, saying he didn't need all of his heavy Maine sweaters in California.

Now, does that sound like a killer?

"Why are you even asking me?" I said disgustedly to Syd. "Silas has been tried and convicted."

"Not by me," Syd said. "Andy, I'm not trying to pick a fight. I'm sick of fighting with you. I really want to know what you think."

"I think he has no motive," I said. "Why would he shoot Dolores?"

"Because she was compiling evidence against him," Syd said. "Maybe he was afraid she'd uncover something."

"But he didn't know where I'd gotten those transcripts," I pointed out. "I never gave him a name. I just said it was someone who worked for victims' rights."

"Andy, think about it. All he has to do is ask someone, and they'll tell him all about Dolores," she said. "Or go to the library and look it up. Or snoop through your desk. It wouldn't be that hard to find out."

I still shook my head. "Maybe you're right, but I still can't see it."

I expected Syd to blow, but she didn't. She just hugged her knees. "Okay," she said softly.

Just then, we heard the noise of a car pulling into our driveway. I went to the screen door and looked out. A dilapidated truck stopped, and Belinda got out. She reached over into the front seat and yanked out a cardboard box.

I hurried out of the house to help her. She greeted me with a frown.

"Took longer than I thought to pack up Dolores's house," she said.

Longer, yeah. And maybe harder, too. Her eyes were swollen, as if she'd been crying. It's funny—it made her look younger, not older. It made me think of Dolores and Belinda as kids. Their ages weren't that far apart. I wondered how close they'd been.

"Dolores left this to you," Belinda said. "She wrote this sort-of will. It's not legal—she wrote it the night she died. Strange, isn't it? Like she knew something would happen."

Belinda shaded her eyes with her hand. "Not that I know what you're going to do with a box of moldy old papers. But to tell you the truth, I'm happy not to have to haul it back to Nevada."

I took the box. "Well, thanks. I guess."

Belinda put one leg into the truck and paused. "Look, I'm not the kind of person who noses around, trying to find out secrets. I lost my sister. It's done. But Dolores was afraid of something. I have a feeling you're mixed up in it somehow. Maybe it's not that Silas. Maybe it's somebody else. Maybe it's a stranger. I don't know. But I'd be kicking myself all the way back to Nevada if I didn't tell you to be careful. Okay?"

"Okay," I said.

She nodded. "Have a good life, kid." She got into her truck, then cranked down the window.

"And a long one," she said.

16//it takes a thief

Syd grabbed the box from me as soon as I came back inside. She'd been listening at the front door.

"Let's look through it now," she suggested.

We started back to my bedroom. But before I'd gone two steps, Mom called out from the kitchen. She was spending more time at home, now that she was fighting with Rachel.

"Don't even think about going to your room until you set out those bags for the rummage sale, Andy," she said. "They're picking them up at five o'clock today. Just leave them by the garbage cans."

"You go ahead and get started," I told Syd. "It will only take a few minutes."

"I can help," Syd said.

"That's okay," I said. "I'd rather tote garbage bags than wade through that material."

Syd grinned and headed for the bedroom. I wrestled the plastic bags through the back door and dropped them by the garbage cans. It only took three trips.

I stopped to grab some sodas for me and Syd, but I'd forgotten one of the bags, which was hiding behind the couch. I put down the sodas and headed to the backyard again.

To my surprise, Bob Treat was standing by the plastic garbage bags I'd already set out. I almost dropped the bag I was holding.

"Whoa, sorry to startle you," he said. "Maybe I should have gone to the front door? I was looking for Silas."

"He's not here," I said. "He's at the nursery."

Bob Treat looked puzzled. "I thought his kid was older."

"For *plants*," I said. "Can I help you?"

"Could you tell him I stopped by? Bob Treat. I'm a friend of his. Hey, are you his kid?"

"Yeah." I balanced on the top step. "Silas said you were let go of your job back in Maine."

"That's right. Thought I'd look for a new job in Napa. Lots of restaurants there. I've got some time to look, though. I'm not in any hurry."

He looked away, then back again. There was definitely something about Treat I didn't trust. With Silas, you got a warm feeling, right off the bat. He looks you in the eye, and his smile is total gold. But Bob Treat looked jumpy and nervous.

"I guess I'd better get back inside," I said.

"Yeah," Bob Treat said. "Well, I guess I'd better go. Nice meeting you."

I waited until he headed down the driveway. And it wasn't until he walked away that I noticed his feet.

He was wearing my sneakers.

Syd nodded when I told her the story. "So if Silas is telling the truth about Bob Treat having a nest egg, why did he steal your sneakers, right?"

"Right," I said. "What's wrong with this picture?"

"Andy, I have a confession to make." Syd bit her lip and looked down. Her eyelashes made spiky shadows on her cheeks. "I asked Dolores to help us find out background on Bob Treat."

"I know, Syd."

"You do?" Syd looked up, surprised.

"It's okay."

"But I said I'd butt out forever, and I rode right over to Dolores's house," Syd said in a burst of confession.

"You were just looking out for me, right?"

Syd looked embarrassed. Or maybe self-conscious. Whatever it was, she was blushing. Her cheeks turned all rosy, and her eyes got brighter.

"Andy," she said, "I know it sounds lame. But . . . I really care about you."

"I know, Syd. You're family."

And then, the crazy girl hauled off and smacked me on the leg. I mean, *hard*.

"Will you stop saying that?"

"What? What did I say?" Confused, I rubbed my thigh.

"Nothing. Let's look at those papers." When I didn't move, Syd smacked me again, lighter this time. "Come on, Beanhead. I don't have all day."

Girls. Why bother trying to figure them out? I pulled the box of papers toward me. We split the papers in half and began to read. Half the stuff was junk: reports on names we didn't recognize, parole records, and court decisions. They could be about people Dolores had seen in the newspaper, or picked off a license plate. Basically, she suspected anyone who was passing through town.

But then, we hit pay dirt.

"Here it is," I told Syd. I held up two papers stapled together. On the top was written FOR ANDY. I scanned the first page.

"Dolores contacted a Web site that gives you information for cash. Treat is an ex-con! He went to prison for larceny. It was his second conviction, too." Slowly, I lowered the paper. "The same prison that Silas went to."

"So they knew each other," Syd said.

"We don't know that," I said cautiously.

"Oh, come on, Andy," Syd said impatiently. "Obviously, Silas contacted Bob when he got out of jail. Bob gave him a job."

"Why would Silas cover for him?" I

wondered aloud. "It doesn't make sense."

"Maybe Bob is blackmailing Silas for something," Syd suggested.

"That sounds like a movie plot, not real life," I said.

"This whole thing is like a movie plot," Syd said with a shudder. "It's unreal."

"Bob is a thief," I said. "He doesn't have any money. He stole my sneakers. Don't you see what this means?"

"He likes Nikes?"

"Maybe he's the bad guy," I said. "Maybe he's the one who was involved with Dolores's death. Maybe he's the phantom burglar."

"And Silas is innocent, right?" Syd asked.

"Exactly," I said, reaching for the phone.

"Who are you calling?" Syd asked.

"The Happy Sole." I listened to the rings.

"Who's a happy soul?" Syd grumbled. "Everyone I know is depressed."

"Hello, this is Andy MacFarland," I said in a slightly deeper version of my voice. "I'd like to speak to the owner, please. Is he or she available?"

"This is the owner. Ned Deedham. What

can I do for you?" The voice was friendly, and had a New England accent.

"A former employee of yours recently applied to our firm," I said. "I was calling for a reference."

"Sure. Who is it?"

"A Robert Treat," I said.

Deedham laughed. "Treat used me for a reference? That's rich."

"Well, he didn't use you, exactly," I said. "But I did discover where he'd worked last."

"Where are you calling from, Mr. MacFarland?"

"Verona, California," I said.

"Well, Mr. MacFarland, from Verona, California, it might interest you to know that there is currently a warrant for Robert Treat's arrest. He happened to clean out my safe when he blew town. Luckily, I had just made a deposit, so there was only about one thousand dollars in there. If he comes back, would you do me a favor and call the police?"

"Oh, my," I said. "That's very bad news. Yes, Mr. Deedham, I certainly will."

"I doubt he'll be back," he said with a sigh.

"Um, do you know Silas Murdoch, by any chance?"

"Sure, I know Silas. If you're asking if I suspected him, he left well before the money was missing. I can't tie him to the theft, but he certainly was a friend of Treat's. That's what I get for giving ex-cons a second chance."

I gripped the phone. "Did you . . . give them jobs, knowing they'd been in jail?"

"Stupid, huh? I got conned, I guess," Ned Deedham said. "When I was young and stupid, I was thrown in the tank for busting up a bar. It followed me for years, till I opened my own place. So I figured I owed the guys a chance. I can't say anything about Silas—he didn't give me notice, but hey, this is the restaurant business. People walk off jobs all the time. But I'd like to get hold of that Bob Treat."

I said good-bye to Ned Deedham and hung up. Silas had lied to me. He hadn't been fired. Neither had Bob Treat. And the owner had known about their prison records!

"What did he say?" Syd demanded.

I didn't want to tell her. I couldn't tell her. She'd read all sorts of things into the lie, and I wanted to think it over first.

"Bob Treat cleaned out the safe of the restaurant when he left," I said. "There's a warrant out for his arrest."

Syd let out a low whistle. "This is heavy. Maybe it's time to go to the police."

For once, Syd and I were in complete agreement.

The police were way ahead of us. They'd already investigated Bob Treat, and they were looking for him.

The problem was that he had disappeared.

"So fast, he didn't even pack," Jeb Mooney, the deputy, told me. "Left his motel room a mess. The owner had a fit."

"I'll bet," Syd murmured.

"What's the name of the guy back in Maine again? I think we should give him a call," Officer Mooney said. "Not to mention the police chief there."

I watched him write down NED DEEDHAM, HAPPY SOLE, BANGOR, ME.

"Do you think Treat had anything to do with Dolores's death?" I asked.

Officer Mooney looked up sharply. "Why do you say that?"

"Because he's a thief," I said.

"Well, it's not his M.O.," Mooney said. "He went to jail for pulling scams and embezzling. That's different from a simple robbery."

"But if he needed money—"

"Sure, he might pull a job." Mooney tapped his pen. "We're just surprised he'd shoot somebody. That's why we want to talk to him."

"Can you place him at the scene?" I asked.

Mooney indicated the desk next to him. There was a sealed plastic bag with a pair of boots in it, the kind of boots everyone wears. I had a pair on, as a matter of fact. I could see the lug sole of the shoe, with its rubber ridges, and the number 10.

"They match the prints outside the window," Mooney said. Another policeman came in the station, and Mooney looked uncomfortable, as if he shouldn't have been blabbing to a couple of kids.

"You can run along now, kids," he said. "The situation is under control."

We walked outside. Syd sighed.

"If there's one thing I'm sure of," she said, "it's that this situation is *definitely* not under control."

17//some justice

When I got home, Mom was banging pots in the kitchen and calling it cooking. Not a good sign.

"What are you doing?" I asked, poking my head in the kitchen.

"Making corn bread," Mom said. She banged a metal bowl on the counter with a *clang*. Then she smashed an egg on the edge, and it exploded in her hand. She started to cry.

"Um, Mom? I may be jumping to conclusions here, but is something wrong?"

She rushed over to the sink and stuck her eggy hand under the faucet. "It's nothing, honey. Just business." She tore off a square of paper towel, dried her hand, then wiped her eyes.

I took a few steps into the kitchen. "Something with Rachel?"

She looked over her shoulder. "Is Syd still here?" she whispered.

"She went home. What's up?"

Frowning, Mom dried her hand on a dish towel. "It's nothing really new, Andy. It's just that . . . we argue now. All the time. The trust we had is gone. I suspect her motives. She suspects mine. It's really hard to come to an agreement. It just got to me, I guess. Rachel was my best friend. I just feel so awful."

"Was? Mom, you can't let this thing with Rachel ruin your friendship," I said. "What are you always telling me about how important friends are? Syd and I have fought about fifty times in the past few weeks, and we keep making up. And Syd is way more stubborn than Rachel. Maybe you just have to make the first move."

Mom bit her lip. "Maybe. She's just so *touchy.*"

"And you're not."

Mom gave me a weak smile. "Touché."

"I thought you said touchy."

Mom laughed. Then she banged a wooden spoon on the counter, like a judge hitting a gavel. "Okay. After dinner, I'll call her. No, I'll go right over there. We're going to make up. Maybe we shouldn't sell the company after all. Our friendship is too important."

"I think that's a good idea," I said. I couldn't imagine life without Rachel in it. And what would happen to my friendship with Syd?

I headed out of the kitchen. Dusk had fallen, and the living room was full of shadows. I jumped a little bit when I saw Silas standing by the bookcase, looking at the titles. He was too far away to have heard us, and what did it matter, anyway?

"You know, I read a lot in prison," he said to me. "But I've gotten out of the habit. Now that I'm out, I like to experience the world, not read about it." He placed a book back on the shelf.

"You can take anything you want, Silas," I said.

His teeth gleamed in the darkness. "Well, thank you, Rocket. I just might do that."

@ @ @

After supper, Silas announced it was his turn to do the dishes. I headed off to my room, and Mom stayed behind to wrap up the leftover chili.

I got thirsty after a while and went back to the kitchen to get a soda. I heard voices, and I stopped outside the door.

It wasn't that I meant to eavesdrop. But when two people are talking in low tones so that you won't hear them, don't you want to creep closer so that you do?

"You really think so?" Mom's voice was soft, worried.

"Maybe I've just seen more of the big bad world than you have, Wendy," Silas said in a gentle, quiet sort of way. "Maybe I'm a cynic. Maybe you shouldn't listen. You should keep that open heart of yours. But if she's hired a lawyer, she's gunning for you. That's a fact. And what I think is that you're a single woman with a kid. I see how hard you've worked for the life you've got. You've got to look out for yourself and Andy."

"So you don't think I should just go over

there? I should let the lawyers handle it?"

"It's what she's expecting. It's what she *wants*. Business is business. I'm sorry to say it, but it's true."

"I guess," Wendy said softly.

I heard a chair scrape, and I bolted away from the door. Why was Silas telling Mom not to reconcile with Rachel? Didn't he tell me that he was trying to get them to reconcile?

And what did Silas gain by keeping them apart?

For one thing, he wouldn't have Rachel whispering in Mom's ear that she'd been taken in by a lowlife.

But there was something else. It hadn't occurred to me before.

Mom had always plowed her profits right back into the business. But if Mom and Rachel sold the company, there'd be a bit fat check for us. So there was another reason Silas might not want Mom to reconcile. Why he might be hanging around. A big reason.

And it had nothing to do with me.

Money.

@ @ @

That night, my e-mail from Syd was short and mysterious.

Meet me at my house first thing. I'll give you breakfast.

"First thing" for Syd means seven A.M. She is an early riser. But I am a more normal human. I got up at eight. And even that was early, for a Saturday. On my way to get my bike, I noticed that Silas had worked in the garden already. All the marigolds he'd planted had been moved. I stopped to look at them.

"They weren't getting enough sun," Silas said, so close to my shoulder that I jumped, my heart pounding.

"You're getting an early start," I said, to cover how jumpy I was.

"Always a good idea," Silas said. He looked tired.

"Maybe you ought to take it easy," I said. "You've made the garden twice the size Mom wanted. You don't have to plant everything all at once."

He gazed over at the plot. "Yeah, I do, Mac. I want it to be perfect when I leave."

"When you leave?"

He nodded. "My two weeks are almost up. Time I was moving on."

That gave me an odd feeling in my stomach. But the funny thing was, I didn't know if I was sad . . . or relieved.

Syd let me in with a short hello. She started toward her room.

"Hey, where's that breakfast?" I asked, trailing after her. "I was thinking pancakes."

"I have some health muffins," Syd said. "But first, I want you to read something."

"Okay," I said cautiously.

We walked into her room. Syd picked up a paper from her desk. "I printed this out this morning. But first, I want you to promise not to get mad."

"I promise," I said.

"No, I mean really promise." Syd's eyes pleaded with me. She was being totally sincere—rare for Syd.

"Okay, I *really* promise. Is this about Bob Treat?"

She shook her head. "I've been looking

for Ham Jernigan," she said in a rush. "I
know you told me not to, but I couldn't help
thinking that he'd be an unbiased witness—"

"Unbiased? He was in love with Pam!" I
said. Then I took a breath. I had promised
not to get angry. "Okay," I said in a quieter
voice. "I'm not mad. What did he say?"

Syd handed me the paper. It was an e-
mail communication from Jernigan to Syd.

*Sorry it took me so long to reply. I run a
company that imports garden statuary, and
I spend a lot of time in Europe.*

*I'll be glad to answer your questions,
Sydney. But not very glad to revisit that
time.*

*Of course I think he's guilty. Pam was
afraid of him. She was saving money so that
she could leave and take Greg. The first
time he hit her . . .*

Slowly, I sat down on the end of Syd's
bed.

*. . . was when he bought a baseball glove
for the baby. Pam laughed at him—not in a
mean way, in a happy way—and he hit her.
Once, he beat her because the vacuum
stripes in the rug weren't neat enough. They*

*didn't go in straight rows. He broke her
tooth, then refused to let her go to a dentist.*

*He wouldn't let her have any friends. We
met by accident, when Pam was buying
geraniums at the nursery where I worked.
We were just friends, but we had to meet in
secret. Pam was afraid he'd get the wrong
idea. But Silas found out and followed her.
He saw us together. I wanted to go home
with her that day. I saw how scared she
was. But she didn't want me involved. She
said it would just make him more angry,
more jealous. It would make things worse
for her.*

*I'll never forgive myself for not insisting.
That was the night she died.*

I swallowed. I couldn't move. And I
couldn't accept what I'd read in that letter.

"I wrote him back," Syd said softly. "I
asked him if he could prove what he said."
She handed me another page.

*Prove it? No. I didn't tape-record our
conversations. I don't have a letter from her,
or even a phone message. I never saw him
hit her. I never heard him threaten her. I just
saw his face that day, when he saw us*

*together, and we saw him. That was
enough.*

*I couldn't tell the stories on the stand,
because it was hearsay, speculation. If you
want proof, I can't give it. I kept track of
him in prison for a while—I knew he was
going to get out. He was paroled. Good
behavior. His cell mate got him a job in a
restaurant he was managing. Some justice.
He's walking around with money in his
pockets, and Pam is dead.*

"His *cell mate,*" Syd said, pointing at the
letter. "It has to be Bob Treat! He lied to
you, Andy. And there's something else."

Syd handed me a file folder. "I took
Dolores's file on Silas from the box. It's
totally complete, transcripts, everything—
except for one thing. Dolores makes a note
here"—Syd pointed to Dolores's handwrit-
ing—"on the last page of the transcript.
Attached is prison info. But there's nothing
attached."

"She didn't get around to it," I said.

"Or Silas took it," Syd said. "Because he
didn't want you to know about Bob Treat.
Because then you'd know he lied. And if you

knew that, Andy, it would place a seed of doubt in your mind. It should place a seed of doubt there. And doubts can grow. He couldn't take that chance."

"Why shouldn't he lie?" I said. "He was afraid I'd turn against him, I'll bet. Look what happened after Belinda spilled the beans at the funeral. Everyone thought he killed Dolores!"

"Maybe he did," Syd said. "We don't know, Andy."

"Bob Treat killed Dolores," I said. I stood up. Hearing Syd's suspicions just made me scared and angry. Even though I'd had my own. "I'm sick of this."

"I am, too," Syd said. "That's why I want it to end. Andy, please, please, just ask yourself this question—what if it's true?"

But I didn't want to ask that. It would open up a black, empty place. A place I didn't want to see.

"Can you imagine?" Syd asked in a hushed voice. "Because you were *there,* Andy. You were around when they fought. When he hit her—"

"Stop it—"

"—when he *killed* her. You were there. Andy, I was thinking about something. About how you jump if somebody comes up behind you. I mean, you actually break into a sweat. I've seen it. About how you hate violent movies, you get sick—not exactly normal teenage guy behavior. You should be lapping those stupid movies up like butter."

"Are you calling me a wimp?" I demanded.

"No! I think you're a totally brave person. Look how you dived into this thing with Silas. You opened your heart, Andy, and that's tough. That's tougher than anything. That's not what I'm talking about. What if, deep inside, part of you remembers things? Terrible things?"

"No," I said. I shook my head so hard, I was sure my brains must have rattled. "There's nothing to remember, Syd!"

She put her hand on my arm. "I'm just trying to help you. Protect you—"

"You're trying to own me," I snarled. I didn't recognize my own voice. "You want me to be your puppet. Think what you

think. That's what you always want. You're
a control freak."

"Please," Syd said. A tear slowly left her
eye and slithered down her cheek. I watched
it in fascination. Syd never cries.

And I liked seeing her cry.

"Can't you see why I'm trying so hard,
you dope?" she asked me. Another tear fell,
and another, and another. "Oh . . . " She
reached for a tissue and swiped at her
cheeks. "I really care about you." She
stamped her foot. "Oh, to heck with it. I
love you, you jerk!"

I felt as though my feet had just turned to
stone. My head was a hunk of concrete. My
tongue was a slab of wood. "What?"

"I don't know when it happened, when I
realized . . . months, I guess. Since last summer."

"But you're the dating machine," I said.

"Why do you think I was?" Syd said, one
corner of her mouth going up. "I was trying
to make you jealous. That's why I hated all
the girls you liked, too. You're so thick."

I felt thick. Syd, my best friend.

My best friend, who I know better than

anyone. I know all her secret smiles, and the fact that sad movies make her cry, but she always dries her tears quickly so that nobody will see. I know the way she looks when she is sleepy, or bored, or the way she gets shy if you give her a compliment, so she changes the subject.

"That's why I can't stand this whole thing with Silas," Syd went on. She wiped at her tears. "You're just being so stupid and stubborn. Such a *Beanhead*."

It was the way Syd talks. She calls me names all the time. I never mind. I just diss her back. But somehow, this time, I minded. Anger ticked away inside me.

But I let her keep talking.

"The thing is, I know why you keep believing in him," Syd said. Her lashes were thick and wet. "It's not because he's your father. Or, I mean, it is because he's your father. You're afraid you're like him. So you want him to be good. But Andy, you're not him. You might have a few stray genes. But he didn't raise you. Wendy did. So it's not like you could ever become him. You're *good*."

The anger blossomed inside me. It seemed to shoot up from my feet, straight into my head. I stood over Syd, looking down at her, and I felt ten feet tall. The traces of tears were still on her face, and she looked soft. Vulnerable.

I thought of all the years she'd taunted me, insulted me, teased me. All the little ways she drove me crazy, flirting with me, letting me think she would never be interested in me because we were just good pals. And maybe because I wasn't good enough, or smart enough, for someone like her.

Never apologize. Never explain.

They know where your soft spot is, and they stick a stiletto in it. . . .

"You really love me, Syd?" My voice was low.

Embarrassed, she nodded.

I bent down so that we were eye to eye.

"I don't care," I said.

18//like father, like son

"We're celebrating!" Silas announced. His head loomed over the sofa.

Then Mom appeared. "Time to get off the couch, potato."

It was later that day. I spent the entire day zoned in front of the TV. Silas had insisted that I take a day off, and he finished up the garden by himself. I was too listless to care. I slouched on the sofa and played a Ping-Pong match in my head between Guilt and Anger.

"Celebrating what?" I asked.

"A decision, Mr. Sad Sack," Silas told me.

"What decision?" I asked. "Did I miss something?"

"I told my lawyer to go ahead with the

contract," Mom said. "So the decision is made. I'm selling the company. The buyer called me today about a new job, so we might have to get packing soon." She looked anxiously at me. "I can fly back and forth for a while, so you can finish out the school year here. We can work it out."

"I don't care," I said. "I'll move with you. I can finish anywhere."

"My two favorite people are moving south," Silas said. "I just might have to rethink Seattle."

Mom blushed and looked down, and I didn't say anything. Silas clapped his hands.

"I say we go out to dinner," he said. "My treat."

"No, my treat," Mom said. "I insist."

"We'll fight over the check, then," Silas said, his eyes twinkling. "What do you say, Mac? How about a nice, thick steak?"

I felt a spurt of annoyance. I suddenly realized that Silas never called me Andy. He always called me Rocket, or Mac. It was like Silas didn't want to know who I really was. He wanted me to be some kid he'd last seen fourteen years ago.

"You know what, you guys? I have this monster headache," I said. "I think I might be getting sick."

Mom put her hand on my forehead. "You don't feel warm. We'll stay home, though. I can cook some pasta."

"No, I think it's just a cold or something," I said. "I'll heat up some soup. You guys go out."

Mom looked at Silas. And something happened inside me. I saw that look, the dependency in it, the *What should we do?*, and I got really, truly scared. Maybe for the first time.

Mom is the most independent woman I've ever known. Sure, she's looking for love, and she's hooked up with some losers. There were the Bad Boyfriend years. But she never let them tell her what to do, or let them push me around. Once, a boyfriend complained to her about my "attitude," and she kicked him out of the house.

She is my mom. And here she was, looking to some guy she'd basically just met, to ask if he thought she should stay home with her sick kid.

That's how good he is.

Get out of my head, Syd! Because I'm right there with you, for once.

Finally.

Yeah, okay. Finally.

Now what?

First, I had to apologize to Syd. I had to tell her what I'd been pushing away all afternoon, trying to fill up my brain with junk TV.

I'd known the truth as soon as she'd spoken it. Leave it to a girl to point out what you've been too dense to see. That for a while now, I'd been comparing girls to Syd, and the girls had been coming up short. I'd go on a date with someone I had a wicked crush on, like Sarah Grommet, and I'd have a pretty good time, and on the way home I'd think, *She isn't Syd.* I'd see something, or think of something, and boom, right on the heels of it would be, *I've got to tell Syd.* For months now, the strangest impulse would pop into my head, like grabbing her and kissing her, right on the lips.

And I saw that every difference between us was nothing, and that she was everything.

Syd and I aren't family. No wonder she'd smacked me that day. We are tied to each other in a much more complicated way. A much more possibly . . . fun way.

And I saw something else. I'd have to grovel like I'd never groveled before. And I'd have to be honest. Because if I wasn't, Syd would never forgive me for being so cruel to her. Honesty was the key.

I hate that.

To: grossgrrl
From: rcktman
Subject: confession

I lied. I lied so bad, Syd. And I'm sorry.

What you told me blew me away. The thing is, it was so mixed up in all the other stuff, the stuff I couldn't face, because it scared me so bad.

I'm still scared about the other stuff. Where I came from, who I am.

But I also know this. Maybe it's the only thing I do know.

I love you, too. I don't know when it happened, either. But it's here, and it hurts, because I know I hurt you, and you might not forgive me.

The reason I was the meanest I've ever been in my life to the person who means the most to me is probably the reason that you shouldn't love me. I'm twisted.

Okay, so maybe I need therapy. But mostly I need you.

Everything is so big right now. I mean, having Silas come here, and all the confusion around it, it fills me up, and I feel like I'm going to burst. I've been bouncing off the walls for weeks, not knowing what I was doing. I was just wanting. I was this big, walking heap of Need, thinking I could make a family. Trying to squeeze somebody into some vision I had of a good father.

I'm an idiot, Syd. I'm a Beanhead. But if you stopped loving me, I'd die.

I signed off. Syd might forgive me. She might not. If I were her, I might blow me off. But at least she would know that I loved her. I knew that now. I knew it because my heart had started to beat again, and it had started to beat for Syd.

Now, it was time to get the rest of my life straight.

I left the house and went to the stairs leading to Silas's room over the garage. He'd left the door locked, but I had the extra key.

I took a flashlight in case Mom and Silas came home early. That way, I wouldn't have to turn on any lights. I would hear the car, and I'd have time to get downstairs, or at least in the backyard. I hoped.

I unlocked the door and slipped inside. I shined the light over the room. It was pin-straight. I wondered if he vacuumed in even rows, like he'd wanted my mother to do.

I searched the room, carefully replacing everything I moved. I checked under the cushions of the couch. In the medicine cabinet, in the drawers. I went through the garbage and the drawers in the child's desk that used to be mine. Nothing.

And I mean *nothing*. No receipts or notes or postcards or even crumpled tissues. It was like nobody lived here at all.

I checked his clothes in the closet, looking through the pockets. I didn't know what I was looking for. I just had to look.

There was a duffel on the floor of the closet, but I could tell it was empty as soon as I lifted it. I unzipped it halfway, but I noticed that the lining was coming away from the canvas backing. I slipped my hand inside.

Bingo. I felt papers. I slid them out, careful not to rip the lining any further.

I spread them out on the floor.

WENDY BELL MACFARLAND was written on top of one page.

It was a printout from a computer. The lettering was small and very fine. I had to lean close to read it by the narrow beam of the penlight.

Mom's bank accounts were listed, along with the account numbers and the amount in her savings. I saw amounts listed, like her mortgage payment, and a payment on a business loan. There was the original price of the house, and how much she still owed. Her annual income.

I turned the page. In neat columns were listed household products, magazines, and general topics like Cooking and Hiking. And weird stuff like Eats Chicken Once a Week and Frequently Buys Hardcover Cookbooks. It listed the radio station Mom listens to and her favorite TV shows. It even said that her dream vacation is to a town called Siena, in Italy, or Lake Louise, in Canada.

No wonder Silas had hit it off with Mom! He'd known what she likes, what she buys, what she thinks about, before he'd even met her.

But I was mystified. How had Silas come up with this stuff?

I riffled through the rest of the pages until I found a handwritten note. It was from Bob Treat.

Here's the guy's name. I checked it out, it's on the level. His company compiles marketing surveys on computers. You know, stuff people fill out for warranties, phone surveys, computer hits. He sells data over the Web. The more you want, the more it costs. Tell him my name.

I turned back to another page. It was information about the offer from ImagiTech to buy out Yellow Crayon. It listed all the financial details.

My hands were shaking as I folded up the papers and slipped them back into Silas's duffel. I knew I should head out, but I was too stunned to move. The information kept whirring and clicking in my head, like a floppy with a defect.

I just couldn't process it. Silas had investigated Mom. He had come here, knowing a million important and stupid details of our lives. No wonder he'd seemed to fit in so well. He had made himself into the image of what we'd wanted. Someone handy around the house, someone who loves to garden and cook. For Mom, someone who likes opera. For me, someone who likes basketball.

I sat staring into his closet. The guy had even bought basketball sneakers like mine.

Whoa. Wait a sec. Those are mine.

I picked up one of the sneakers. It was the pair I'd sent to the rummage sale.

The pair Bob Treat had stolen.

But Silas has smaller feet than I do. Doesn't he?

I remembered back to the police station. To the boots I'd glimpsed through the plastic, lying on their side. Bob Treat's boots, the police had said.

But those boots were a ten. Two sizes smaller than mine. Bob is tall, like me. We both have big feet.

I took the sneaker in my hand. I returned downstairs, crossed the patio, and opened the back door. I turned on the light in the family room, the enclosed porch that Silas had painted.

In the corner was the footprint Silas had left in the wet paint that day with his work boot.

I placed my sneaker next to the print.

Silas's foot was at least two sizes smaller.

19//if the shoe fits

I heard a noise at the front door, and I spun around like an idiot. Should I pitch the shoe, hide it under the sofa, or run back up to Silas's and put it back in the closet?

While I was still spinning, I heard someone call my name. It was Syd!

I hurried to the front door and unlocked it. Her face was grim, pale.

"I know you don't want to see me," she said.

"I—"

She walked past me. "I won't stay long. I just wanted to tell you this one thing. This last thing."

"Syd—"

"Please, Andy!" Her jaw was set. I knew she was fighting tears. "Let me just get this out. My mom came clean tonight. You were right about something. She did meet with Silas. He contacted her. He told her that he wanted to avoid trouble between your mom and my mom, so he wanted my mom to know that *your* mom had hired her own lawyer for the sale. Mom didn't believe him, but then the lawyer called her—"

"Syd, wait, I—"

"I'm almost finished. The lawyer was *Bob Treat,* Andy. I mean, they used another name, but the description fit perfectly. I think Silas wanted our moms to fight so that they would sell the company. Maybe he has a plan to get the money from your mom somehow. I don't know, Andy. You don't even have to believe me. But I just had to tell you, anyway."

Syd turned. She started toward the door. I had heard everything she said very clearly. But I didn't, at that particular moment, care about it. All I could think about was the fact that Syd hated me. I could see it in her face, in the way she held her arms against her sides. She couldn't forgive me for being so mean.

And who could blame her?

"Syd!" I said. She stopped, her hand on the knob. "Did you get my e-mail?"

"What e-mail?" She didn't turn around.

"Oh." How could I tell her in words how I felt? It had been so much easier to write it.

"So, do you want to print me out a transcript, or do I have to go all the way home and read it?" Syd asked in a muffled voice.

My smart-aleck Syd was back.

I took a breath. "It said that I lied to you before. I do care. I was just so mad at everybody—mostly you. I don't even know why I was mad, except that life isn't fair and gave me a liar and a murderer for my father. It said that I was wrong. And . . . it said that I loved you, too." I said that last part in a rush. I had to get it out fast, because if I didn't, I wouldn't be able to say it at all. "I've loved you for months, only I didn't see it. I guess I'm always going to play catch-up with you. You're way smarter."

I waited. Syd still didn't turn around. I didn't know why I loved such a stubborn, aggravating girl, anyway.

Then I saw her fingers slip off the door-knob, and I started to hope.

"That last bit was overkill," she said flatly.

She turned around to face me, and a little more hope tiptoed into my heart. Still, Syd didn't look very welcoming.

"You really hurt me, Andy," she said.

"You don't know how much I wish I could take it back," I said. "Do you think you can forgive me?"

She smiled that soft smile that has a tendency to hit me right at the knees. "I don't know yet," she said. "But I might consider it."

That's when I kissed her for the first time. It was exceptional. It pushed the concept of kissing into a whole new category for me.

But that's all I'm going to say about it. First of all, it's none of your business. It's between Syd and me. And second of all, it didn't last very long. We had work to do.

"Syd, you were right about Silas," I said. "I found out tonight that he's been conning us for sure. And I have proof."

"I knew it," Syd said. "The whole thing just didn't smell right."

I held up the sneaker.

"Um, speaking of *smell,* why are you waving your old sneaker in my face?" Syd asked.

I told Syd about the sneaker, and how Silas had switched shoes with Bob Treat so that the police would think the shoe prints belonged to Treat, only his feet were bigger, my size. I explained how I thought *Silas* was the one who had murdered Dolores, and now he was wearing shoes too big to disguise his real shoe size. And I remembered a couple of other things, too—that Silas had said to me, *Who told you that—the crazy lady with the newsletter?*, which meant that he had investigated Dolores, because I'd never mentioned the newsletter. And finally, I ended on the day that Dolores had seen Silas in the yard and called him the devil. She was already afraid of him. Maybe he'd threatened her. That's why she was leaving town.

I had to talk fast, because it was getting late. I didn't think Mom and Silas would be back so soon, but I couldn't take any chances. Syd followed it all. Didn't I say the girl was a wizard?

"I'd better put this back, I guess," I said, indicating the sneaker.

"I'll come with you," Syd said.

"Okay," I said. "But we have to hurry."

We ran lightly up the steps to Silas's apartment. Syd held the flashlight while I put the sneaker back.

"How are we going to get the police to investigate?" I whispered. "I can tell them the sneaker story, but—"

"Maybe you should take the duffel bag," Syd suggested.

"It's still not proof that he's working a scam," I said. "He hasn't taken one penny from Mom. I bet the worst they could do is scare him off. I want them to nail him."

"What about Bob Treat?" Syd asked suddenly. "It's awfully weird that he disappeared without taking his stuff. And he wouldn't let Silas switch shoes like that." Syd's eyes were wide in the dim light. "What if he didn't disappear? What if Silas *killed* him? Oh, Andy, what are we going to do?"

"I know we need more proof than a pair of shoes," I said.

"We need a body," Syd says. "But poor Bob is probably fertilizer somewhere."

Then I heard the sound of a car. I ran to the window.

"They're back!"

Syd switched off the flashlight. "What should we do?" she whispered.

"Wait," I said. "Silas might go in the house for coffee or something."

I held my breath and watched as Silas and Mom chatted by the back door. I prayed Mom would invite him in, and that he'd accept. But maybe she wouldn't, because she knew I wasn't feeling well and she wouldn't want to disturb me.

So what would she do if she found out I wasn't even home?

Silas started to do that old male head-bob that meant he was about to plant one on Mom. But she ducked her head and took a step back.

Way to go, Mom!

She smiled, so she wouldn't offend him. Then Silas put two fingers to his eyebrow in a salute, turned, and ambled back toward the garage.

"He's coming!" I said.

Syd looked around wildly. "What should we do?"

"The window." I was already moving. "It's a drop down to the gardening shed roof, but I think we can do it. The roof is flat. And there's a ledge you can balance on."

I eased the window up and looked down. "It's not far. But I could lower you."

"It will take too long. I can jump it."

Syd crawled through the window, balanced on the ledge, then hung on to the sill and dropped to the roof below.

"It's a cinch!" she whispered.

I crawled out and balanced on the ledge while I eased the window down behind me. I dangled for an instant, then let go. I landed softly next to Syd, praying Silas didn't hear the thud. Squirrels aren't that big around here.

"We'd better get off this roof," she said next to my ear.

The shed was small, so it was easy to just

hang over the side and let go. The ground was soft from Silas raking and putting in topsoil for the garden.

The garden . . . Silas was so dedicated. He'd gotten up so early to move those marigolds. What a perfectionist—they'd seemed to be in the sunny spot, to me. And today, he wouldn't let me work in the garden at all. He'd wanted to finish it himself. . . .

I touched Syd's arm, and we moved to the shadow of the pine tree in the corner.

Remember how you said Bob was probably fertilizer?" I asked her.

She nodded.

I jerked my head toward the garden. "I hope you feel like digging," I said.

20//dig it

First, I eased a shovel out from the shed. It would be better if we dug one at a time, while someone kept lookout.

I hadn't forgotten about Mom. The last thing I needed was her sounding the alarm because I wasn't home. If I go out, I always leave her a note.

So I told Syd to wait, and I skulked down the driveway, around to the front door.

When I walked in, Mom had her hand on the phone. "There you are!" she said, relieved. "Where were you? I was just about to call Rachel, and you know how much I don't want to do that."

"I felt better, so I went over to Syd's for a while," I said. I gave a big yawn. "But now

I'm really beat. I think I overdid it. I'm going to hit the sack."

"Good idea, sweetie," Mom said. "It's been a real roller-coaster last few weeks, hasn't it?"

Mom, you have no idea.

I stuffed pillows under my covers, just in case Mom peeked in on me. Even though she hasn't done that in about a thousand years.

Then I climbed out my window and tiptoed down the driveway again. I'm telling you, I could make an awesome thief.

Syd jumped as I came up. We both were pretty spooked, I guess. *You* try preparing to dig up a dead body.

"Ready?" I whispered.

"Ready," Syd said.

We edged along the fence to the far side of the garden, where Silas had replanted the marigolds. Luckily, this part of the plot wasn't visible from Silas's window.

"I just have one question," Syd whispered. "What do we do if we find something?"

"That's easy," I said. "We throw down the shovel and run like heck—"

"Straight to the police station," Syd finished.

Syd melted away to act as lookout, and I began to dig. It was a dark night, with only a quarter moon. That was good. I didn't want to actually see what I was looking for. I just wanted to know if it was there.

After a while, my arms started to ache, and Syd appeared at my elbow at just the right time. Silently, she took the shovel, and I made my way back underneath the pines, where I had a good view of Silas's staircase.

We traded places two more times. I could tell that Syd was getting tired. I was, too. We had dug a rectangular hole down about three feet or so. Maybe four. But it was just in one portion of the garden. We couldn't possibly dig the whole plot up. It would take all night. Longer.

Syd must have had the same thought. "Maybe we should just go to the police," she said when I appeared to take over the digging. "This is starting to feel kind of hopeless."

"Let me try one more time," I said. "Then we'll talk about what to do."

Syd nodded. She moved off, just a shadow in the darkness. I started to dig again. I was sweaty and tired and ready to give up when my shovel hit something.

It wasn't something hard. It was soft.

I scraped away some dirt. Something pale gleamed against the black earth.

A bare foot.

"Hey, Bob," I whispered. My heart was pounding so loud, I put my hand over it as though I could quiet it.

The voice behind me was so soft, for a minute I thought I'd imagined it. The funny thing was, for the first time in my life, I didn't jump. I didn't shift into full-adrenaline mode. It was like I was used to him sneaking up behind me, and it didn't spook me anymore.

"Almost looked like he was sleeping," Silas said. "All death is gentle, son. Real gentle. The soul just . . . gives up. So don't be afraid. . . ."

21//father's day

My first thought was Syd. What had he done to her?

I opened my mouth to . . . what? Scream at him, shout at him, demand what he had done. . . .

But I got smart, and I shut up. Maybe he hadn't seen Syd at all. Maybe she was still out there. I hoped so. I had to hope so. Because the idea that Silas had done something to her made me want to pass out, or hit someone. Hit *him,* as hard as I could.

"Looking for your mom?" Silas asked. "She went to bed. Must be fast asleep by now. She was tired. Maybe a little confused. Because I kissed her good night. And she liked it, Rocket. She liked it a lot."

A lie. And the way he said it, you'd never

know it. You'd never know it at all.

"Keep the lies coming, Silas," I said. "See if I ever believe another word that comes out of your lying face."

He moved quicker than a breath. He punched me in the mouth. I fell down in the dirt. I tasted dirt and blood and blind rage.

"I didn't think it at first. But you take after your mother," Silas said. "She didn't listen to me, either. Back off, I'd tell her. Shut up, I'd tell her. There's got to be a man in the house, Rocket."

Silas looked over at the dark windows of the house. "And now there will be."

"You killed my birth mother," I said. "You won't get her, too."

"What are you going to do, boy?" Silas put a foot on my chest and held me there, against the ground. "You tell me, now. What are you going to do?"

I grabbed his ankle and yanked, sending him backwards, just a bit off balance. Enough to get to my knees and grab the shovel. I swung it at him, and hit him in the leg.

He grabbed the shovel and threw it

across the yard as though it were a twig.

"She was cheating on me," Silas said. He pressed his foot against my chest again and forced me down. This time, he added pressure.

"The tramp! She was cheating on me, Rocket. She was breaking up my home! I had a right! Jernigan was stealing my wife!"

"No, he wasn't," I said.

It wasn't just that I'd read Jernigan's words. It was strange. I knew the truth of it, I knew it in my heart. As though that shy, gentle person, my birth mother, was whispering in my ear. *Believe in me. Believe. Keep talking. . . .*

"How do you know?" Silas spit out furiously. "How did any of them know? Lawyers and juries and judges! They weren't there. They didn't know what she'd done to me. How she'd tortured me and betrayed me."

"She was afraid of you," I said.

He looked baffled for a minute. The man had his boot on my chest, pressing me down into the grave of a man he had killed, and he was *surprised* that his wife was afraid of him!

"I gave her everything. Nice house. Clothes. Anything she wanted."

"Right. You're the victim, Silas."

"You know, I thought there was me in you," Silas said, pressing against my chest. It hurt. It was hard to breathe. I could hear ragged breaths coming from somewhere, and it was from me.

"Now when I look at you, I see her," Silas said. "You're just as stupid as she was. How do you know she didn't cheat on me?"

I saw movement behind him. Syd rose up out of the darkness.

"Because Ham Jernigan is gay," she said.

Surprise crossed Silas's face, and he half turned. "A *fag?*"

In a lightning move, Syd hit him full in the face with the shovel. I threw myself forward and tackled him. Howling with pain, he stepped back on Bob Treat's bare foot. He lost his balance and fell—on a stake that marked where we'd planted the zucchini.

It must have hurt. He let out a yell like a wounded rhinoceros.

Syd hit him with the shovel again.

"You are *so* politically incorrect," she said.

22//epilogue

To: grossgrrl
From: rcktman
Subject: you were right; I was wrong

You asked me to say it again, so here it is. I was wrong. Okay? Can we drop it now?

And, okay, you were right about something else. I guess I was afraid I had Silas in me. That's why I couldn't accept that he was a murderer.

But you were right again. (You're loving this, aren't you?) Maybe I have his eye color gene. But he didn't bring me up. Maybe all that cosmic stuff is right, too. It was all meant to happen—not my mom dying, that wasn't fair no matter how you look at it— but maybe I wasn't meant to be raised by them. I ended up with the mom I was meant to have.

We could debate all this stuff forever. And we could fight about it. You know how long the two of us can hold a grudge. Which reminds me, you haven't officially forgiven me yet.

Maybe we should stop talking about murder and betrayal and lies. Silas is back in jail where he belongs. The Moms decided not to sell the company. They've even forgiven each other. So everything's back to normal. Sort of.

Except that one really major thing has changed. Things between us can't stay the same.

So what I was thinking was . . .

Maybe we should go out on a date. A real date, on a Saturday night, where I pick you up, and we wear sorta nice clothes, and we go to the movies, or to get something to eat.

Whaddya say?

To: rcktman
From: grossgrrl
Subject: date

there's only one thing that really changed. you do realize this—that if it's an official date, and I wear something nice . . . that you have to pay?

and I'm not talking cheeseburger, buddy boy. i'm going for the special. i think i deserve it, don't you?

xoxo, s

Get caught in a web of danger!